case closed

also by patrik ouředník in english translation

Europeana: A Brief History of the Twentieth Century

CASE CLOSED
PATRIK OUŘEDNÍK

translated by alex zucker

dalkey archive press
champaign / london

Originally published in Czech as *Ad acta* by Torst, 2006

Library of Congress Cataloging-in-Publication Data

Ouredník, Patrik.
[Ad acta. English]
Case closed : a novel / by Patrik Ourednik ; translated [from the Czech] by Alex Zucker.
  p. cm.
Originally published: Ad acta, Prague : Torst, 2006.
ISBN 978-1-56478-577-0 (pbk. : alk. paper)
I. Zucker, Alex. II. Title.
PG5039.25.U74A64 2010
891.8'635--dc22
                              2009048555

Partially funded by the University of Illinois at Urbana-Champaign and by a grant from the Illinois Arts Council, a state agency

This translation was subsidized by the Ministry of Culture of the Czech Republic

www.dalkeyarchive.com

Cover: design and composition by Danielle Dutton, illustration by Nicholas Motte
Printed on permanent/durable acid-free paper and bound in the
United States of America

This translation is dedicated to P. K.

1

1. e4 e5 2. f4 exf4 3. Bc4 d6 4. Nf3 Bg4 5. 0-0 Qd7 6. d4 g5 7. c3 Nc6
8. Qa4 Be7 9. b4 h5 10. b5 Nd8 11. Nbd2 Nh6 12. e5 Ne6 13. Ba3
Nf5 14. d5 Neg7 15. Rfe1 Ne3 16. Qb3 Rh6 17. exd6 cxd6 18. Ne4
Bxf3 19. gxf3 g4 20. b6 a6 21. Be2 Ngf5 22. Qb2 f6 23. c4 Kf7 24.
Rac1 Rg8 25. Kh1 h4 26. fxg4 Ng3+ 27. hxg3 hxg3+ 28. Kg1 Rgh8
29. Bf3 Qxg4

2

It was summer, the sun smiling, the trees piously, if in vain, exuding oxygen, sparrows flapping among the boughs, dry pigeon dung dropping from baroque moldings, a stink wafting from the sewers. Viktor Dyk sat on a bench in front of the park entrance, warming his old, life-weary bones as he readied his cane to crush a beetle walking past. *Carabus granulatus*, the granulated carabid, or ground beetle. Dyk was aware that he had to go about it gently, lest he bust his back with some reckless movement. Propping the cane with his left hand roughly halfway along its length, he was about to crush the bug with his right when a young person of the female persuasion appeared in front of him in a short skirt and deep-cut blouse. She was braless, and her face was red from walking fast.

"Excuse me, how do I get to the Academy of Fine Arts?" Under her arm she held a large green portfolio, bound with gray ribbon in six strategic spots.

Dyk raised his eyes and looked her up and down. Seeing that she was attractive, he took on the expression of a kindly, wise old man, cocked his head, and said, "Pardon me?" despite having heard each and every word.

"How do I get to the Academy of Fine Arts?" the female repeated.

"What on earth would you want there, little lady?" asked Dyk jauntily. "You're pretty enough as it is."

The little lady grinned uncertainly.

Dyk regarded her thoughtfully as he sought to recall the hair in the crotch of his late wife, Anna.

The little lady paused a moment, then pointed her hand and asked: "This way?"

"Oh no," said Dyk. "You need to go back to Roosevelt, take a left, and then . . . hold on . . . the third right."

"I thought it was around here somewhere," said the young lady hesitantly.

Dyk gave a kind grin. "Miss, I've been living here fifty-five years, and I may not be able to walk much anymore, but my memory, praise God, still serves me well." He tapped his finger on the handle of his cane. "Left on Roosevelt, then the third right."

"Well, thank you very much," said the young lady, and she set off in the direction indicated.

Dyk watched her a while, then turned his eyes away and poked the ground with his cane. The beetle had left to tend to its own affairs.

She could have lifted her skirt, mused Dyk. Just for a second, what harm would it have done her? There was no one else around. She could have shown me her pussy and I would have told her how to get to the Academy. Maybe she wasn't wearing panties either. What harm would it have done her? Third right. Serves her right.

Not that Dyk had anything against beetles. At one point, in the depths of the last century, he had even had a collection of them and gone to the park every Sunday with a pair of tweezers, a pincushion with various sizes of safety pins, and a bottle of ink with a screw-on top. Most of his collection consisted of ground beetles and pine sawyers.

Nor did Dyk harbor any particular antipathy toward female students of fine arts. It was people in general that bothered him. Although it was true, the younger they were the more irritating he found them, in accordance with the simple rule that the more recent their date of birth, the longer they would pollute the earth with their presence. Old people were no more appetitlich than the young, but they did have one mitigating quality: they wouldn't be kicking around for long. Not that Dyk had any illusions: for every—

"Why, hello! What have we here? Mr. Dyk! Gorgeous weather, isn't it? And how are you doing?"

A fat, pink-cheeked retiree with a scarf on her head—a rare thing these days—and a half-empty, or rather half-full, plastic bag sat down heavily on the bench next to Dyk.

"Oh, you know, Mrs. Prochazka." Dyk discreetly slid over.

"Have you heard? Mrs. Horak was hit by a car."

"No! Is it serious?"

"Serious or not, she's dead from it, dead as a doornail. Supposedly she staggered home, opened the door, and bang! she was gone. She couldn't breathe, poor thing, and her eyes were wide open."

Not that Dyk had any illusions: for every dearly departed, 2.2 specimens of the new brood came rushing into the world.

"The eyes of the dead lend their sparkle to the stars."

He said.

"Proverbs 8:125."

He said.

Dyk had a habit of pulling pronouncements out of his noggin and dressing them up with fraudulent, usually biblical, sources. Long ago he had come to realize that repeating what someone else had once said was considered the utmost expression of intelligence in his country. At one time, in the days when he still collected beetles, he used to declare ownership of his pronouncements ("as I always say"), but he never got any response except an awkward smile. Until one day it occurred to him to add "Book of Ruth 6:4"—and lo and behold, eyes lighted up all around, women's in appreciation, men's in envy. Since then, he had done so every time. "Night is the harbinger of the morn. Leviticus 10:2," he said, rising from his chair as he left the office party. "Dig in the sand and ye shall find yourself. Ecclesiastes 5:17," he urged a female colleague whom he had set his sights on. "The father calls out in a mighty voice, Beware, but the son hears not. Gilgamesh, Canto Three," he consoled a neighbor complaining about the behavior of his adolescent offspring.

Nor did it fail to have an impact this time. Mrs. Prochazka snorted in glee and gazed at Dyk admiringly.

"You always know how to put things," she said.

"Sum them up," she corrected herself.

"Concisely," she specified.

"I was talking about you with Pavel just the other day," she added. "You know, my husband. Mr. Dyk always knows how to put things, we were saying. And he knows so much!"

"Oh?" replied Dyk absently but by no means impolitely. Why be unpleasant? It was bad enough just looking at her.

"Pavel was saying you would get along with Teddy. You know, our son. He's got a business now, renting boats at Revolution Bridge. And he knows so many interesting things! Mostly from the past, all sorts of battles and wars and where things were signed and so on. If he wasn't already in business he could easily teach history. Maybe at a prep school or at university."

Another old-timer came puttering up to the bench. He had a beret on his head—a rare thing these days—and a half-full plastic bag in his hand.

"What gorgeous weather!" chimed the old-timer in the beret. "How's everyone doing?"

Dyk scowled. If it kept on like this, his favorite bench would turn into an annex of the retirement home.

The old-timer in the beret dropped down beside Mrs. Prochazka, who slid closer to Dyk, who discreetly slid away.

This is a regular Paleolithic site, he thought resentfully.

"By the way, have you heard? Mrs. Horak was hit by a car."

"Mr. Dyk and I were just talking about it. Poor woman. Supposedly she staggered home and her eyes were wide open. Mr. Dyk says that the eyes of the dead lend their sparkle to the stars."

"Hm," said the old-timer in the beret.

Without the source being cited, the statement was utterly worthless.

3

Adolescents were the worst. Formerly known as *youth*, the vanguard of our society, striding forth in the footsteps of their fathers, who themselves had only managed to make it as far as the rear guard. After the change of regime, *youth* had been replaced by the less momentous and more modern-sounding *teen*, which was better suited to the new age. "Are you pro-teen?" No! "Do you take kindly to teens?" No! "Do you have anything against teens?" Jawohl!!

When Dyk was in grade school, the term *teen* generally signified a juvenile delinquent who cracked you on the head for no reason at all as you peacefully made your way down the school stairs; who grabbed you by the scruff of the neck like a rabbit and shook you till the change your mother had given you that morning to buy a crescent roll spilled out of your pocket. When Dyk himself passed into the category of teen, there were other, higher-ranking teens above him who cracked him on the head, hissed at the Lolitas who worked at the nearby textile plant, and squeezed blackheads out of their noses with their index fingers. And notwithstanding the fact that Dyk did blossom successfully—not that it was really his own doing—he acted so stupidly that he looked back on it to this day with a mixture of disgust and disbelief: he had punched younger pupils in the head and dug his thumbs into their throats as they peacefully made their way down the school stairs past him, hissed at the Lolitas from the nearby textile plant, nonchalantly squeezed out blackheads with his index fingers, and carried a greasy comb around in his ass pocket.

Teenagers! Adolescents! Yuck! That calf-eyed look! Those squeezed-out faces! That herdlike confidence in their own uniqueness! That stupidity dating back to the depths of larval prehistory! That dinosaur-size ego, tamed by the merest whisper of Sieg Heil, Long live communism, or Think different!

And as soon as those illiterates figure out how to fuck, you have to close your window even in the steamiest heat, so great is their desire to notify the neighborhood of their orgiastic triumph.

4

Dyk's bench was located on a square that was practically rural, bounded on one side by a modest though baroque church and on the other by a former stables, now the Andy Warhol Museum. The stables used to belong to a hunting château, now the Academy of Fine Arts; under the last regime they had housed the Museum of Workers' Resistance. The Academy itself was hidden behind the first line of trees in the park, which took up nearly a quarter of the district. Inhabited for the most part by longtime residents, the neighborhood was distinguished by its serenity, an increasingly rare thing in the new millennium, when every yokel around was trying to elbow his way into the EU. The only blemish of note on the neighborhood's pastoral atmosphere was a few apartment houses occupied by Gypsy families. The Gypsies, also known as Roma or jigs, spoke a strange and incomprehensible tongue, which disturbed the otherwise largely peace-loving attitude of the citizens of non-Gypsy origin, also known as Gadjos or pastyfaces; the encroachment of linguistic alterity gave them the unpleasant feeling that the world was either too big or too small.

Abutting the church on the park side was a small graveyard, which, remarkably, had withstood both communism's enthusiasm for dismantling and early capitalism's zest for construction. Word on the street was not for long; a Canadian firm had proposed to build a three-story structure with a terrace on the site. Given that ancestral respect is a natural reflex for Canadian developers, the building was to rest on columns, leaving the graveyard intact. The second and third floors would house a supermarket, or überstore, with the fourth floor occupied by offices, a florist, and a funeral parlor. The terrace would be planted with linden and ailanthus trees, in whose shade the citizens could look down on the church roof, and equipped with a playground, complete with jungle gyms and a sandbox, thereby achieving a symbolic symbiosis with the graveyard on the ground below: Play, play, you'll die anyway. The Canadians had also pledged to spruce up the graveyard, replacing the damaged crosses and tombstones with new ones, and in general to do their utmost to accommodate both deceased and still-thriving Praguers alike.

There was some graffiti on the cemetery wall. A few predictable statements (*M. loves J.*, *Roman can kiss my ass*, *If you're reading this you're a loser*) had been supplemented by two more ambitious ones: one a Cartesian inquiry (*Mila's a whore, David loves Mila, is David a whoremonger?*), the other cautiously optimistic (*Leave your phone number or e-mail if you like to read Verlaine*).

Every now and again some overeager tourist devoted to pop art and the avant-garde would invade the square, but this was a fairly rare event. The museum was off the beaten tourist paths and few foreign visitors were acquainted with the fact that Andy Warhol was actually Czech, or actually Slovak, which is the same thing, at least for Warhol, a native of Pittsburgh. In fact, most people who have gone on to make something of themselves in this world have been of Czech origin: Sigmund Freud, Madeleine Albright, et passim. Slovakia, though now split off, can lay claim to other famous

Near-Czechs, tender souls in agile frames; Andrej Varhola was one of them.

The neighborhood also had the park to thank for its peaceful reputation: too public for prostitution, too far away from downtown for drug dealing. If not for the growing number of maniacs in the morning and early evening who engaged in the activity known as Djo-Ging, which had replaced calisthenics by an open factory window with a view of the factory grounds, at first glance there was little to suggest that the wheel of history turned here too.

The only really obvious evidence of historical evolution could be found on an artificially elevated platform in the park. Where Generalissimo Stalin once towered, a victim of the Twentieth Congress of the CPUSSR, there now stood a colossal pendulum, illustrating the movement of time in duly equal parts mechanical and symbolical. In the previous century's next-to-last year, promoted by the mass media to last, an LED panel had been temporarily installed beneath the pendulum, ticking off the seconds that separated the city from the century's alleged end. Thus, between the first of January and the last of December 1999, 31,536,000 seconds had slipped away from the former monument to Generalissimo Stalin. Since the century's alleged end, another 111,758,400 of them have slipped away, each like the next, all of them equally astonished. But today, friends, today we can discuss the last century impartially, with cooler heads and some perspective, the generalissimo having taken his place alongside Pericles and the atom bomb, joining Assyrian trestle guns and the Battle of Crécy's wooden cannons in the chapter on the evolution of military technology. Not that the new century's seconds are slipping away any more intelligently than the last one's, God forbid, but perhaps, Dyk thought hopefully every now and then, perhaps this one would be the last. After all, the experiment can't go on forever. As a former attendee of lectures in the Department of Natural Science and a subsequent expert on the life of the ground beetle, Dyk was aware that nature is full of alternatives. Perhaps one day the ants will have their say. Or the jellyfish. Wouldn't that be a scream. Despite the outcry from environmentalists, the shrinkage of the glaciers, and the decline in the sperm count of civilized species, there's been nothing so far to suggest that this is the end, but a hundred years is a long time, never mind a thousand. There's been nothing so far to suggest that this is the end, just the same old sewer of wars, famines, idiotic murders and idiotic murderees, but jellyfish aren't as dumb as they seem, and their lust for power is every bit as passionate as anyone else's—just look how blissfully and single-mindedly they gobble up everything that floats past their mouths.

5

And behold, here comes another one poking along. A man like a mountain, brimming with health, the kind of idiot that even diseases shun. In his hand he held a plastic bag.

"Is this great or what?" he called out cheerfully.

"Ah, Mr. Krebs!"

Mr. Krebs stood in front of the bench. "So, what gives, retirees? You think I could squeeze in, now that I'm one of you?"

Mrs. Prochazka attached herself to Mr. Dyk, hoping that Mr. Platzek—the man in the beret—would slide the other way, leaving her between her favorites, Mr. Dyk and Mr. Krebs. What she appreciated most about Mr. Dyk was his education; Mr. Krebs, on the other hand, was a regular barrel of laughs.

Her move paid off. Mr. Platzek nearly toppled off the bench as the enormous Mr. Krebs planted himself between him and Mrs. Prochazka.

"What a life!" said Mr. Krebs. "You buy a strainer, it leaks. You get it fixed, it doesn't strain! Ha-ha!"

Just like I was saying, thought Mrs. Prochazka, tingling with delight.

Then she said: "You're all fun and games as usual, Mr. Krebs, but meanwhile our Mrs. Horak was hit by a car."

"Is she dead?" inquired Mr. Krebs with delight.

"Supposedly she staggered home and her eyes were wide open. Like the stars, Mr. Dyk here said."

"The stars? How so?"

"They were sparkling. I mean it must have been a shock. Her head was all covered in blood."

"Can't knock down a wall with your head, the way to go's to piss it down. Ho-ho!"

"Why, Mr. Krebs!"

6

Mrs. Horak's death wasn't a result of the accident. The car was innocent. It barely grazed her. Mrs. Horak fell down, banged her knee, tore her stocking. Ranting and limping, she made her way home. Once there, she turned on the gas, opened the oven, and stuck her head in. They say that women, particularly in old age, rarely resort to suicide, and when they do, they think long and hard about their decision and as a rule they choose less radical means than men do. But statistics provide only an imperfect picture of an individual's life: in this respect Mrs. Horak defied sexual categorization. She'd had enough, she had had it up to here. Her sister, children, grandchildren, doctors' appointments, the blonde in the grocery store, drivers who didn't respect crosswalks. Even Mr. Dyk, who you could talk about anything under the sun with, who knew so many things, and who in nice weather she would sit on the bench or walk in the park with; why, she had even invited him over for Sunday lunch a few times, she a widow, he a widower, she going on about Tony, he about Anna, you know how it is. As she put her head in the oven she chuckled: Now who was Mr. Dyk going to sit on the bench with?

The first thing the firemen noticed when they got to the apartment a few hours later—by which time the entire floor smelled of gas—was the mess in the bedroom and the living room, contrasting sharply with the scrubbed and tidy kitchen and their idea of old ladies' cubbyholes in general. For in this regard as well, Mrs. Horak failed to conform to the criteria of her gender. Anthropologically speaking, the attitude of women toward chaos is preventive: they clean so as not to have to. The logic may be debatable, but it does get results. On the other hand, the attitude of men is curative: they clean only when they feel directly threatened by chaos.

Mrs. Horak, it seems, was the representative of a third, in-between category, as yet untreated by the social sciences.

We shall see later whether and to what extent these statistical incongruities influence the course of our story and the fates of our other protagonists. In any case it spurred the firemen to call in the police without delay. Which they would have done regardless; this, however, enables us to evoke a promising atmosphere of tension, thereby strengthening the dramatic line. The firemen may not give a damn, but our readers certainly do.

And one more thing caught their eye: some damp clumps of hair and fur and some sticky splinters of soap in the bath. Whose hairs they were, who had bathed in the tub and when—the firemen would leave that to more qualified individuals.

7

With an irritated wave of her hand, Mrs. Prochazka brushed away a bee that had confused her artful curls for an exotic flower.

"They're like flies this year," she groaned.

"You know what Einstein said?" put in Mr. Platzek, balancing on one buttock. He felt spurned; it was obvious to him that if he wanted to remain a full-fledged member of the collective, he needed to say something clever. "If bees were to disappear, mankind would only have four years left to live."

"Well then, instead of inventing the atom bomb he should've come up with a way for us to get by without bees. Am I right or aren't I?" chuckled Mr. Krebs.

"That's what they said on the radio," insisted Mr. Platzek.

"I got stung by a bumblebee once," said Mrs. Prochazka. "They say bumblebees don't sting, but they do. My hand was so swollen you wouldn't believe it."

"If I were a bumblebee, I'd sting you somewhere else! Ho-ho!"

"Oh, go on with you, Mr. Krebs!"

"It has to do with the pollen. If it wasn't for bees, there wouldn't be any flowers or trees or oxygen. There wouldn't be anyone to collect it. The pollen."

"If it wasn't for bees, the Vietnamese would collect it! Ho ho ho!"

Mr. Platzek, offended, fell silent. Mrs. Prochazka took advantage of the pause and turned to Mr. Dyk.

"Don't you have something to say, Mr. Dyk?"

"Silence is a form of speech," replied Mr. Dyk.

Mrs. Prochazka looked puzzled.

"And the reverse." He couldn't resist.

"The reverse?"

"Speaking is just another form of silence."

Mrs. Prochazka felt her head begin to swim.

"You think?" she asked uncertainly.

"I think, though I don't want to. The thought is stronger than I."

8

Vilém Lebeda sat in his office at the Linden Street police station reading the *Rough-book of the Czech Language,*[*] hoping to gain some knowledge of the language of the street, which due to his bourgeois upbringing had been denied him until now. He was disappointed. The book came across as shallow and unconvincing, but it had been recommended to him by his boss, whose mistress had given it to him for his birthday, and Lebeda took it as a professional and social obligation to thumb through it all the way to the end.

Located in a peaceful district of peaceful inhabitants, the Linden Street police station was a peaceful place. The majority of cases it handled were lacking in drama: stolen wallets, stolen purses, stolen umbrellas, stolen retail goods, stolen traffic signs from intersections, stolen pipes from scaffolding, stolen benches from the local park, stolen jeans off courtyard laundry lines, stolen wipers off of cars, and stolen tires. Only rarely was there occasion for a dynamic intervention of the sort that would justify lights and a siren: the arrest of an exhibitionist harassing schoolgirls in bloom or a drunkard threatening citizens with a stolen brick. When a real crime did occur, it was usually an unfortunate accident, a husband banging his wife's skull off the kitchen floor, failing to realize how fragile a

---

[*] *Šmírbuch jazyka českého: slovník nekonvenční češtiny* (Rough-book of the Czech Language: A Dictionary of Unconventional Czech) is an actual book by Patrik Ouředník.

vessel a woman's brainbox is, or some pimpled retardate accidentally shooting a friend while showing off his new gun. Every now and again some idiots stabbed a Gypsy and every now and again some Gypsies stabbed an idiot, but in that case there was nothing to investigate, they just called an ambulance, typed up a report, selected *Save* from the pull-down menu, checked it for errors, and printed it out in triplicate on the antediluvian printer dominating the hallway that led to Vilém Lebeda's office.

Lieutenant Lebeda held the rank of security corps officer and chief inspector of the Linden Street police station, which apart from basically regular service brought with it *(a)* "additional benefits," which in the parlance of the ossifers charged with writing ordinances indicated a service uniform or other appropriate attire, as well as accessories intended for its modification or associated with maintenance of equipment to the extent required by the terms of discharge of duty; *(b)* "special perquisites," namely, *(b1)* the right to use one station telephone line for the purpose of prompt communication regarding the assignment of service tasks, and *(b2)* the use of a service vehicle for the discharge of duty or in connection with it and for personal use for the purpose of ensuring immediate availability.

In addition, for a monthly supplement of 1,810 crowns, Lebeda also carried out the function of "covert operative," which pleonasm signified an inconspicuous and perceptive person who prowled around the district, eavesdropping on gossip and taking note in his notebook of any suspicious behavior. The covert operative was deployed solely on a needs basis, in cases where the criminal activity was presumed to be more or less spontaneous and collective, and precisely one such case had crossed Lebeda's desk in the past month, in a greasy folder of uncertain color. The case was called Damage of Advertising Surfaces in Public Spaces. In the past six months the city's metro and streetside postering surfaces had been flooded with signs of an active anticapitalist, antiadvertising campaign—whole posters x'd out in black, as well as graffiti both general (*Down with advertising, Ads lie, Citizen, don't be an ass, Pay the unemployed*) and specific (*Women are not goods, This washer will wash your brain, Bud won't make you wiser*), while billboards along the D1 and D2 highways had been brutally assaulted. Advertising firms were demanding compensation, though they should have been glad that anyone had even noticed their postered asininity, and the ministerial adviser for the environment had gone on the radio to address this unacceptable vandalism, which not only did nothing to help improve the environment but in fact was irreparably damaging it, since paint and spray paint both contained all sorts of chemical crap. Thanks to painstaking work, criminologists ascertained that the first antiadvertising storm troops had sprung up in pockets in the late nineties, although they only began to cause real damage with the onset of the new millennium. In the initial phase, Lebeda had been charged with working up a typology of antiadvertising pests. Which was no easy task: the storm troops, it seemed, were extremely diverse in ideological orientation, from Pacifists Against Advertising (PAA), Trotskyists Against Capitalist Aggression (TACA), and Environmentalists Against Polluting the Planet (EAPP), to Young Christians (YC) and Women for Women (WW); not to mention various anarchist elements, who changed their obscure organizations' names on a regular weekly basis, and the sprayers, who confused the civil war against advertising with the production of art, albeit their own. Just last week Lebeda had come across a group called the Castrati, who painted billboards with huge pink Ken dolls, each with a word balloon that invariably declared, "I am a eunuch and proud"; a careful graphological analysis revealed that the group numbered two active members. One of the hotbeds of the advertising pests, it seems, was in Lebeda's district, where there was an unusually high number of disfigured ads, whether underground, in one of the six metro stations, or on the surface.

Apart from the defaced ads, Lebeda was nominally occupied at the moment with a raped student of fine arts, two arson attempts at the local retirees' club, and one suspicious suicide. On his own initiative, he had also developed an interest in a forty-year-old unsolved murder near Bear Rock, in the Ore Mountains. In which matter, however, he had no jurisdiction; apart from the fact that the case was closed, it was under the authority of the Chomutov police.

Vilém Lebeda set aside the *Rough-book* and stared into space a while; whereupon he lifted his 110 kilograms with a sigh, took his jacket from the peeling coatrack in spite of the summer's unusually high temperatures, tossed it over his shoulder, groped around in his right pocket, lit his pipe, and strode out of the office.

9

Miss Reis had been raped as she hurried to an appointment with Professor Pelan at the Academy of Fine Arts. Bad luck had dogged her all day. The train from Hradec had been delayed, she had taken the tram one stop too far, and, to top it all off, she had the wrong address; in her mind the Academy was near the square with the baroque church by the park, but the last time she had been in Prague was as a little girl, and apparently the Academy had merged in her memory with the Museum of the Workers' Resistance, now the Andy Warhol Museum. Fortunately, she had been helped by a retiree, sitting there warming his old bones and listlessly poking the dirt with his cane. The appointment was scheduled for eleven o'clock and now it was seven minutes to. She was embarrassed about being late, Professor Pelan had freed himself up to be able to meet with her at the recommendation of a friend of her mother's who had been a witness at the wedding of his sister, but he certainly didn't have time to waste. Miss Reis walked down Hollar Lane, turned left on Roosevelt Avenue (previously Soviet Heroes Street, formerly Stalin Boulevard, ex-Siegstrasse, erstwhile Woodrow Wilson Road, once-upon-a-time Emperor Way), and after three hundred meters or so crossed the street and headed for Puklich Street. She had barely gone twenty meters when a perverted individual garbed in a black havelock jumped out from a dark alley, grabbed her by the hair, stuffed a smelly cloth in her mouth, dragged her behind some trashcans, pulled down her skirt, tore off her panties, and shot his despicable seed into her.

10

"It hasn't been this hot since I can't remember when," said the boat rental man. "The last time was in 1898."

"You don't say."

"It wasn't much better in '46, but still."

"I wasn't even alive yet."

"What about me? I wasn't born till ten years later. The Hungarian revolution, you know."

"I wasn't even conceived yet."

"It didn't used to get this hot."

"Well, at least the sun is out."

"In 1815 the water dropped three meters. But in 1876 they raised the embankment. Nowadays it's much higher."

"Nowadays they're also building a lot."

"They used to build even more. But not so high."

"These modern buildings are awful. Apartment blocks and so on."

"People want to live right. You know what the population of Prague was in 1501?"

"No, I don't."

"Me neither, but I read it somewhere."

"Probably in the paper."

"But I remember it was a lot less."

"Of course, times were different then."

"The year after that, Columbus discovered Honduras. 1502."

"You don't say."

"And in 1815, when the water dropped in Prague, Napoleon lost at Waterloo."

"That's in Holland, right?"

"Belgium. But it didn't used to get this hot."

"Well, at least the sun is out."

11

Once Anna died, collecting bugs in parks lost its validity as a legitimate excuse to break away from the family every Sunday, under the pretense of pursuing a noble hobby. For some time afterward, Dyk devoted himself instead to idleness and reflection.

Anna was a concerned mother, no doubt about that. The first month after giving birth she didn't get a wink of sleep. Whenever Dyk Jr. squealed, she would run into the kitchen where the massive old crib stood (60 crowns at the bazaar) and pop a bottle in his mouth. Whenever Dyk Jr. kept quiet too long, she would run into the kitchen and put her ear to his mouth to make sure that he was still breathing. Meanwhile she was panting so loudly that no matter how hard she tried she couldn't hear a thing; at which, seized with vague apprehension, she would blanch and give Dyk Jr. a gentle pinch on the arm; he would start to squeal and Anna, relieved, would pop a bottle in his mouth.

As a result, Dyk Sr. didn't sleep either, and developed a serious grudge against his offspring.

The first word Dyk Jr. was indisputably heard to utter was *myuum*, a scrummagy synthesis of the words he heard most often: *mama*, *yum*, and *coo-coo*. Feeling justifiably proud, he contorted his face in concentrated expectation of praise. Anna, however, having mistakenly interpreted his exclamation as a cry of pain, scurried around the kitchen in confusion for some time, until the trembling and disappointed Dyk Jr. burst into full-on screams. To which Anna responded by laying him in his crib and covering him with three layers of quilts. And if, perhaps, until this point Dyk Jr. had believed in the adequacy of articulated expression and the real essence of objects, he quickly got over it. He was sweating like a stuck pig.

Dyk Jr. was not even five years old when Anna died. Dyk Sr. would have been happy to stick him in a foundlings home, but it wasn't so simple. For one thing, there weren't that many orphanages out there, and for another, 0.5 of an orphan isn't really the same thing as a whole one. City Hall granted Dyk Jr. priority placement in nursery school and enlisted the caretaker of the building next door to pick him up from school every day and wait with him for his father to come home from work. As it happened, the caretaker's name was also Anna, which fact does not contribute to the transparency of our story; let's call her Anna the Second.

Beneath the vigorous gestures and obligatory informing on tenants, Anna the Second hid a pious soul and a certain theological erudition. "God is the true and best parent of orphans," she told Dyk Jr., semiseverely, semisentimentally, in the first weeks after he lost his mother. "Such is the glory of the house of God that by comparison all men's homes are as one slapped together from clay, or brittle as a snail's shell." Dyk Jr. didn't know the words *truand*, *reeof*, or *somzar*; he had the impression she was speaking a foreign language. When he added to that the fact that she had appeared in his life out of nowhere, he came to the conclusion that *Auntie* was most likely insane; but as long as she bought him a roll on the way home from school every day, he was willing to keep his suspicions to himself.

Anna the Second knew what she was talking about; she too had lost one of her parents as a child. Her father perished on the southern front in World War I. The announcement of his death was conveyed by a one-armed soldier by the name of Tonda Kubel—"Kubel Tonda here. I got news about Franta but it ain't exactly good"—and an unusual announcement it was. It occurred on December 24, 1915, when a Benedictine priest showed up to serve as the regiment's sawbones. As Kubel told it, Anna the Second's father, patriot, pacifist, and anticlerical, had angrily declared: "Do we need a priest here, friends? God doesn't exist. If I'm wrong, let him show himself by destroying this lethal weapon which I wield in my right hand." And brandished his rifle over his head like a club.

At that very instant, Kubel said, a bullet came sailing in from enemy lines, shattering the handguard of her father's rifle and sliding straight into the blasphemer's skull. A course, conceded Kubel, it's easy to see the finger a God in all sorts a things. For instance, ever since the day lightning hit the cottage of my momma's widowed sister-in-law an took out half the roof she won't have nothin to do with her. But, continued Kubel, this thing shook us bad, I swear. Everyone that was there was shook, includin the new priest. He was pale all over, I tell yuh, hands shakin an everything, which the rest of us thought was strange, seein as he was the only one that shouldn't of been surprised, right? But I hope the Good Lord's forgiven Franta. He wasn't a bad man.

Anna the Second was there when Kubel told her mother this bizarre story. Her mother heard him out to the end, whereupon she swooned and fainted. Kubel kneeled down to her limp body, swiftly undid her bodice, and told Anna the Second to go in the other room and play.

In the end Dyk Jr. came to like his crazy aunt, and he would gladly have gone to live with her rather than his father, but he knew these decisions weren't up to him. Often, after she left, he would sob pitifully in an attempt to express his position as forcefully as possible, and perhaps also in the hope that his father would take a roll out of his shabby briefcase in order to console him. But nothing of the sort happened; Dyk Sr. flopped down in the one easy chair they possessed, gave his offspring a weary look, and said:

"Just keep crying, son. It'll leave you less to pee."

Whereupon he stood up and went to the kitchen to make himself some coffee.

Eventually, then, Dyk Jr. made up his mind—proceeding unwittingly from the psychologically verifiable fact that verbalization of trauma is the first step toward healing the situation and acquiring the necessary social confidence—to resort to a more civilized form of communication. So he swallowed his tears and more or less articulately inquired:

"How come Auntie's not here anymore?"

But even that didn't work.

"Because. She would have turned me in."

Objectively speaking, this reply made no sense. Setting aside the fact that Anna the Second's purview was solely confined to the building of which she was the duly appointed caretaker, Dyk Sr. had nothing in particular to hide from the regime. The significance of his response was therefore purely subjective, but all the more generous for that; it's good to rouse one's heroism from time to time, even if only hypothetically.

For Dyk Jr., though, it was further proof that language was useless, being utterly unfit for interpersonal communication.

Dyk Sr. wrung several acts of intercourse out of the situation, provided by female colleagues who were moved by his premature widowhood. They also repeatedly offered to take Dyk Jr. out on Sundays, to the zoo or someplace else, but in that respect they failed; Dyk Sr. had no intention of mixing his sex life with his family life. He figured out fairly quickly that the best way to deter adepts of substitute motherhood was to portray his son as a retard. "Apart from a few wholly exceptional cases," he explained to the most persistent of them, "you don't have to have a degree in biology to tell a living creature from an inanimate object: a living creature breathes, grows, and so on. The trick is with the exceptions. My son, for example. He grows, yes; breathes, of course; but that's about all." Whereupon Dyk Sr. would mention the trickle of saliva flowing practically uninterruptedly from his son's mouth, his hydrocephalic head and frozen stare. He only had to adopt the proper tone, resigned and vacantly sad, to elicit another wave of sympathy for himself and cash it in for one more fuck.

A year and a half later, when Dyk Jr. began his compulsory school attendance, his mother's older stepbrother, a retiree with nothing left to sink his teeth into, started to take an interest in the boy. But his uncle didn't bring him rolls either, instead forcing Dyk Jr. to borrow old picture books, reeking of mold, which he lent to him with an air of ceremony and consequence, and which Dyk Jr. would have to return the following Saturday and respond to his uncle's unpleasant questions asking what they were about.

Fortunately, his uncle died soon after. He suffered a stroke while trying to board an overcrowded tram, and spent the last three months of his life in bed. He was cared for by a niece, fifteen generations removed, who hoped to inherit his apartment. Dyk Jr. went to see him once, on a compulsory visit; his uncle lay in bed, rolling his eyes and feverishly wiggling the fingers of his right hand. He clearly enjoyed Dyk Jr.'s visit; it was a rare moment, his niece remarked, when his uncle tried to speak. His lips scarcely moved; the sounds leaped from his mouth like flying fish.

"Hawoo?" he asked.

"How is school?" translated his niece.

"Oo ee fa yeh?"

"He wants to know if you're reading faster yet."

"Aaooeh . . . aaee . . . dihs."

"At your age he was already reading Dickens."

Dyk Jr. stared in fascination at his uncle's gaping mouth, wondering whether he was able to eat beans. Why beans of all things he had no idea.

"Well, we'll be on our way," his father said from behind him.

A few days later, his uncle was in the ground. Time is a great healer.

Yes! It flows, it rushes, it strides, full of majesty and calm assurance. The widowed Dyk slowly grew old and bald. Every now and again he would bang a female colleague, every now and again he would visit the local library or the theater, more infrequently the movies or the pub. Dyk Jr. meanwhile grew taller and hairier, and nearly made it all the way to his graduation exam. But in the end he wasn't allowed: a few weeks before the fateful date, his class went on a field trip to the Monument to Peace, and Dyk Jr. and three of his classmates ducked away to a pub in which they reduced themselves to a state of intoxication. On their way back, his classmates began shouting "Russkies, go home!" at the top of their lungs (Dyk Jr., as was his wont, remained gloomily silent); the most hardened of them even screamed out a ditty slandering the world socialist system under § 98 and § 104 of the criminal code at some Girl Pioneers returning from their own visit to the monument:

Here we are, young Pioneers,
our slits are still as tight as ears.
Once we get to be big Commies,
we'll be whores just like our mommies.

All four wound up in jail and missed their graduation exam. Thus does time flow, mysterious and merciless. Dyk Sr. only rarely left Prague. He read and went to the theater, the movies, the park, or the pub. Every now and again he would bang a female colleague, but the opportunities grew less with the advancing years; if not for office parties, God knows whether any woman at all would still have put out for him.

Thus does time flow, inexorable and unstoppable, healing all wounds: dies adimit aegritudinem hominibus. Every now and again a war broke out somewhere and another one ended somewhere else, every now and again a new trend popped up, and every now and again some newer one squeezed it out. Dyk Jr. came home from investigative detention, finally began to earn some money, picked up some chick somewhere on the town, and moved out to the suburbs somewhere with her.

Thus does time flow, whimsical and permanent: damnosa quid non imminuit dies? Dyk bought a TV and a new washing machine and asked himself whether human existence had any meaning. What had he got out of life? His youth was gone, Anna was rotting in the grave. His fiftieth birthday was just around the corner, he suffered memory loss, insomnia, and oppressive dreams when he managed to sleep. I'm disappointed, yes, disappointed in myself. I can feel my mental energy rapidly seeping away.

Insomnia as a symptom of depression, never mind that; that was easy to fix under normal circumstances: Just lose all hope in the future and you'll sleep like a log. But we're talking about the days when Dyk had yet to reach maturity and still harbored the illusion, however feebly and irrationally, that life could be influenced in a positive way every now and again.

It wasn't any better from a physical standpoint, either: arthritis, infirmity, sweating spells, corpulence, depilation of the underarms and genitals, reduction in testicular volume, increasingly unreliable erectile function, thin ejaculate: nec quae praeteriit, iterum revocabitur unda cunta. At night he groaned, panted, and moaned; in the daytime he suffered aches in various parts of his body—back, kidneys, left knee, one or the other elbow, stomach, gums, fillings, even his fingers.

Faced with his increasing nothingness (for even nothingness can increase), Dyk made up his mind to act. But how? Rebuild his beetle collection, establish warm relations with his son and his son's fiancée, join the firemen's club? Visit the Adriatic coast? Take up gardening? Become a dissident? Give the big city the boot and withdraw to the womb of Mother Nature? Sign up for language school and learn to speak Italian?

In the end he decided to write a book. Not that he believed writing books was especially useful, but he had a sneaking feeling that he could write a good one, the question was what about? At first he thought an atlas of beetles or a collectors' guide, but neither of those seemed literary enough. He tossed around the thought of his story with Anna for a while, but arrived at the opinion that it wasn't a story at all. Next he considered writing a historical novel (wavering between Albrecht von Wallenstein and James Cook), but eventually concluded that it would be presumptuous to tackle something so complex. He also weighed the idea of a novel set in the present, exposing the troubles of modern-day society against a backdrop of humor, but he soon came to believe that the modern era was no less troubled than any other, and instead began to think about some sort of family saga, with the intertwining fates of several generations; in the end he shrank the number down to one or two. One day in a cabinet in the entry hall he discovered some of his father's notebooks from school, along with two crude children's drawings, a tattered copy of de Amicis's *Heart*, a blurry photograph of smiling soldiers in elegant Wehrmacht uniforms, an identification tag, a dagger with the inscription MEINE EHRE HEISST TREUE, and a set of dentures that had belonged to Sergeant Pfeifer, his father's oldest friend and adviser. Pfeifer fell in the Battle of Stalingrad, and Dyk's father had lovingly removed his teeth, feeling that the presence of dentures might somehow detract from the fallen soldier's heroism. Having survived the Russian campaign, Dyk's father deserted during the German army's retreat, and for the remainder of the war he hid with relatives in Moravia. In 1945 he returned to Prague and hanged himself. Dyk kept the photographs, drawings, notebooks, tag, and dagger; he hesitated a moment when it came to the dentures, but then, unable to think of any good use for them, he threw them away.

12

Vilém Lebeda walked down Old Post Office Street and headed for a vegetable stand to buy some tomatoes. A few days earlier, he had decided to take a stab at making his own tomato juice. The rotten tomatoes were carefully tucked away underneath the good ones, an effect of the last revolution; under the old regime they didn't bother with such formalities. Lebeda bought two kilos of tomatoes from a grumpy man with dirty nails and then went on his way. Two- and four-legged beasts, dubious creatures of various genders and faiths, moved sluggishly through the sunbaked streets. The retirees' club resided on the ground floor of a nondescript prewar apartment building on Halek Street.

At the entrance to the building hung a display case half filled with death notices. The remaining space was taken up by announcements ("*Meetings and fun every Wednesday and Saturday*"), one hoary photograph of a group of smiling retirees in a garden restaurant somewhere, a sign in capital letters reading RETIREES, FORWARD!, and two quatrains of verse. The first served as a caption to the photograph:

> *There is no country that is small,*
> *as long as its ideals stand tall.*
> *Never mind that it's in tatters,*
> *it's what's in its head that matters.*

The next quatrain was posted in a framed space titled *News of the World*. It was pinned up underneath a year-and-a-half-old article, torn from a newspaper, reporting on the successes of the allied forces in Afghanistan:

> *The world's worse off than a speechless brute,*
> *everything gleams with weapons that shoot.*
> *Everyone carries machine guns around,*
> *in today's world there is no common ground.*

Lebeda stepped inside and headed toward a door with a sign that read *Retirees' Club Here: Ring and Enter*. He Rang and Entered. He found himself in a spacious entry hall.

"You aren't allowed in here," said a croaky voice attached to a face in the corner across the room. "Only retirees are allowed. If you're new, you'll have to fill out a form." A tiny old man in a shabby sportcoat of ancient cut peered at Lebeda suspiciously.

"Mr. Puml?"

"That's me."

Lebeda started to take out his ID, but then thought better of it.

"Excuse me, there's just something I'd like to ask about. Confirm, actually. About the fire. There's all sorts of talk going around, you know how it is. My mother sent me. It's about Mr. Dyk. He is one of your members, isn't he?"

"Mr. Dyk? Oh, yes. He's a widower, though. Been that way for years now."

"I know. Mr. Dyk is my uncle. My mother is concerned about him. You know, people say all kinds of things."

"So she's his heir?"

"That's right."

"Aha."

"It nearly ended in tragedy, from what they wrote in the papers."

"Mr. Dyk has a son, though."

"That's right, yes."

"Didn't turn out too well. His son, that is. Not well at all."

"I know."

"I never knew he had a sister."

"A brother. They had a falling-out. It's been a while."

"Aha. So that's how come."

"That's right."

"Do you know him? The son, I mean."

"Remotely."

"They say he drools."

"That's right."

"And his sister-in-law's his heir?"

"First the son, of course. Then my father. At least that's what she thinks. My mother."

"Families, ah, yes."

"You know how it is."

"Vultures, every one."

"Still, it would be a shame to do without them . . ."

"Mr. Dyk is a writer."

"That's right, yes."

"Real smart fellow. Did you see those poems outside? I wrote them. Mr. Dyk said that they would make even a prize-winning author proud."

"They're very nice. Evocative."

"So Mr. Dyk's sister-in-law sent you? His brother's wife?"

"Yes. The fire gave her a scare."

"Scare?"

"Let's say a fright."

"The police were here."

"Yes?"

"They even took the butts from the ashtray."

"Have they found anything yet?"

"Please. They're not even really looking. Who cares about retirees nowadays?"

"You're right about that."

"Only the vultures."

"Still, it would be a shame to do without them . . ."

"There were three of 'em. They took all my butts."

"People around here are saying maybe it wasn't an accident. Two times in one year . . ."

"You better believe it wasn't. But the cops'll never solve it. They'd have to know how to treat people. Talk with 'em. Offer 'em smokes. I sit around all day here. Three times a week. Thursdays I do paperwork, Wednesdays and Saturdays meetings and recreation. And all of it volunteer. But who cares about retirees nowadays?"

"What about the other tenants? Are any of them elderly?"

"Mrs. Naiman. On the third floor. Widow. But she doesn't come here. Not only that, she makes fun of us. Going around all made up like she was still thirty, the slut."

"Anyone else besides her?"

"Mr. Hroznata on four, but he's always drunk. And his wife, but she can't walk. Broke a crutch the other day. Her, I mean; not him. He's still spry, the lush."

"There are two apartments on every floor, is that right?"

"Not every one. The ground floor yes, but no one lives there. On the second floor there's some Ukrainians or whatever they are. And Mrs. Kalousek, but she's a long way from retirement still. Three and four have only got one apartment each, though. Twice as big, of course."

"It happened Saturday night, is that right?"

"That doesn't mean a thing."

"What do you mean?"

The old man scowled.

"I mean what I said."

"Maybe it was just an accident. Most of your members are smokers, aren't they?"

"I don't know. Never counted."

"I smoke a pipe."

"Hm. Not me."

"And what about the women? Do you have any female members?"

"Four and a half."

"Four and a half? How so?"

"Four come regularly, one only once in a while. Helenka."

"Mr. Dyk was friendly with Mrs. Horak, wasn't he?"

"That's right. But she's gone now."

"I assume the police asked you for a membership list."

"I keep my papers in order."

"I'm sure. It's obvious from the bulletin board that someone here really cares."

The old man softened a little.

"So you really just smoke a pipe?"

"Really."

"I forgot to buy some today. Cigarettes. But I can't leave, in case somebody comes."

"I can go get you some if you want. I've got time. What do you smoke?"

"If I had the money on me, I'd buy an American brand. Marlboro or whatever."

"I'll bring you some back."

"But I won't be able to pay you."

"Please, don't even mention it."

"Know what? You buy me the Marlboros, I'll give you what I've got, and we'll call it even, for my time."

"Sounds reasonable."

"Does, doesn't it? Well then, you better get going."

Just as Inspector Lebeda with his sack of tomatoes is heading for the nearest smoke shop, someone is breaking into Mrs. Horak's sealed apartment nearby. The door handle clicks, the door swings open, an unidentified man enters and heads straight for the bedroom without a moment of hesitation. On his last visit here, he had noticed a new-looking shoebox sitting on top of a chest of clothes and bedding; for reasons we'll keep to ourselves for now, he hadn't had a chance to examine its contents last time. As a result, he now commits an illegal act, risking a serious run-in with the police, in order to do so.

This unidentified man may equally well be an unidentified woman; in which case our readers will have to adapt the previous two sentences: her, she, she, she.

13

"Why, Mr. Dyk, you've got new shoes!" declared Mrs. Prochazka, as if Dyk didn't know it. The old ones had ended up in the trash: the left shoe had begun to flap open wider and wider and the right shoe was too small. He'd passed by two stores he knew from the old days, but neither of them was there anymore; the first had been replaced by a twenty-four-hour convenience store, the second by a night-club, otherwise known as a "nightspot." In the end, he'd had to go six tram stops farther down the line to find shoes. A pair of shiny round-toe clodhoppers of domestic make for 2,450 crowns. They came with a booklet titled *A Few Common Guidelines for Proper Footwear Use.* (Why "common"? Dyk had resigned himself to such inept usage years ago.) Here he read, among other things, that appropriate hygiene and changing his socks every day would contribute to the health of his feet, that at temperatures above 50°C footwear would be critically damaged, that leisure footwear could also be used for walking in slightly modified natural environments, and that in rainy weather footwear should be changed often. The leaflet was emblazoned with four logos: *Dermatex, Deska E, Lorenzo*, and *Gloria Line*. (Aha! So that's why "common"! They put their heads together.)

"They really suit you! And you didn't even brag!"

Dyk slid his foot toward Mrs. Prochazka. "Step on it."

"Excuse me?"

"Step on it. New shoes should be christened, you know that."

Old memories flashed through Mrs. Prochazka's mind and her voice just melted. "You think? Well, if I dare be so bold . . ."

"Please, do dare!"

Mrs. Prochazka lovingly ran her old clodhopper over Mr. Dyk's new clodhopper, letting out a titter.

"You're going to have a smudge there."

"Better a smudged shoe than a smudged brain," quoth Dyk. "Evang—" he stopped himself just in time.

"Do you think I should wipe it off? With a handkerchief, you know?"

14

Writing novels turned out to be much less fun than collecting beetles. After jotting down some dramatic situations, intended to give
the story a framework, and sliding the first page of his future novel
into the typewriter, Dyk's inspiration abandoned him. He tried
various approaches: *I was born November 15, 1926. As my uncle
told it, the streets were full of rotting leaves as a mist gathered outside
the hospital windows.* Or: *That day I was celebrating my tenth birthday. Mama had baked a cake, and even Papa managed to muster
a smile.* Or: *Before the war we used to go to X every summer. My
father was an avid fisherman, and in X he had found true paradise
on earth, in the form of Pulkava Creek, whose waters were teeming
with trout.* Or: *"Where did he wander off to now?" his mother sighed,
gazing anxiously at the old-fashioned kitchen clock.*

Here we should add, especially for younger readers, that in those
days, when Dyk was writing his first (and, as it turned out, last)
book, writers had to fend for themselves. There were no guides, let
alone writing workshops. No *How to Be a Writer in Three Months*:
"Lesson One: Choose an appropriate theme; Lesson Two: Use a
dictionary to find unusual adjectives; Lesson Three: Don't be
afraid of metaphors; Lesson Four: Write colorfully and compel-
lingly; Lesson Five: Authorial perspective on epic passages will
clarify characters' psychology better than the wittiest dialogue."
No, nothing of the sort, just painful creative solitude, a typewriter,

a ribbon that constantly jammed, and a special hard-rubber eraser that invariably rubbed right through the one typo on each ploddingly pecked-out page.

To which we must add the traditional handicap facing every Czech writer: they take their books seriously. As a result, Dyk wasted loads of time in search of a fundamental idea to weave unobtrusively through the moral truths which were to resound throughout his novel.

But he didn't give up. After each unsuccessful attempt he began anew, and a year and a half later his novel saw the light of day. Novella, actually. In first-person form. About a city boy, with the first down on his chin, who joins up with the partisans in October 1944 and falls in love with the beautiful maid in the mill, whom the miller himself—failing to grasp that a new era is dawning, an era belonging to youth—has also set his sights on.

It was a sad story. The miller, jealous of Dyk, reports the partisans to the Germans, who chase them through the woods, decimating the squad one by one: first the bowlegged Batik, then Kantor, whose glasses break as he runs away, then the hulking Ruda, who worked for the railroad before the war, then Hryzal, Pepa, and Véna the miner (for reasons of class consciousness, the story—see below—could hardly be lacking a miner), and finally, on May 6, 1945, his beloved Tonka, the maid in the mill, felled by a stray bullet. After the war, the miller became chairman of the local agricultural cooperative, but that isn't in the book. Actually, the miller isn't in the book at all, having been replaced (see below) by a landowner, a member of parliament for the Agrarian Party. In real life it was unclear whether the partisans were reported by the miller, who was jealous of Dyk, or the miller's wife, who was jealous of Tonka. In the book, Tonka, the maid in the mill, is presented as a virgin (until the moment, in Chapter Six, when she gives herself to her first love, as the first spikes of grain are pushing up from the fields), while in real life the miller uncorked her when she was thirteen, and from then on went back two or three times a week, to make sure all his equipment was working the way it should. For that matter, maybe it wasn't the miller's wife who reported them but somebody else entirely; it could have been anyone, really—the village was full of sharp-eyed informers all just waiting for the right opportunity. The local women despised Tonka, parading around the village square jiggling her breasts, and the men couldn't stand Dyk, who a few years earlier had paraded around the village square in his city clothes acting slick. Dyk's father had never made a secret of his pro-German views—believing the Thousand-Year Reich to be the only sensible alternative for nations with no will or culture of their own, and being aware of the danger threatening his country from the direction of the muddy East—and the fact that his son joined the partisans only proved that city folk had no respect for anything, beginning with their own parents. The fact that his father had joined the Wehrmacht was something Dyk didn't tell the partisans, though they probably knew and didn't care; in reality they were just a bunch of guys who liked to dress up in army gear and tramp around the woods playing cowboy—though the risks were quite real, even if they themselves underestimated them—stuffing themselves with fresh bread every morning, supplied to them by the local baker at unchristian prices. For that matter maybe it was the baker who reported them; given that Tonka had never put out for him, he was even more jealous of Dyk than the miller was.

Dyk finished his book in the midseventies, but for a long time couldn't bring himself to send it to a publisher; he had some idea how bad it was. If not for the fact that he always mentioned his writing to the women at work he intended to bang, he would probably never have done it. Three months after he finally did, he received a letter from an editor at a publishing house insisting on a few revisions. Véna the miner was added to the ranks of the partisans, the miller became a landowner and Agrarian Party MP, and the narrator's father, to whom the initial manuscript had devoted only a few trivial, fragmentary mentions, was promoted to a Communist Party member who died just before the war as the result of a brutal police interrogation. The editor gave Dyk the choice of three different pen names and included a contract for him to sign. In the end the book was published under the name Viktor Jary, to no response except for the obligatory reviews in the obligatory papers. In payment Dyk received a whopping 14,800 crowns, two-thirds of which went to the plumbers who were redoing his bathroom and the rest to the dentist who was paring down his teeth.

Nevertheless, life is full of the unforeseen and chance is a form of necessity: After the fall of the hated regime and the inauguration of a free and independent state, Dyk was sought out by some people from TV who asked him to cowrite and appear in a documentary series titled *Fates*; someone from the publishing house had betrayed the true identity of Dyk's father to a producer. The dramatic content of Dyk's life—"The father a Nazi, the son a partisan; later an inconspicuous pencil pusher and unsuccessful writer"—intrigued the creators of the new historical epoch, who had been called upon to undertake a scrupulous revision of the past.

15

Mrs. Prochazka yawned, stepped clumsily into her slippers, cracked her knees, snapped her spine into place, and headed into the bathroom. Blew her nose in the sink, spat out some spit, leaned toward the mirror, plucked some hairs from her chin with a tweezers, and rubbed the gunk from her eyes. Poured a slimy green liquid into a red cup and rinsed out her mouth. Thought a moment about whether or not she needed to urinate (having gotten up three times during the night), then gave the flush chain an absentminded tug. Went into the kitchen, cooked up her morning mush, pulled a pastry of vaguely bunlike shape from a plastic bag, walked into the living room, went to the window, opened it wide, and looked out. Mr. Platzek sat on the bench in front of the park, talking to a man she didn't recognize. Mrs. Prochazka rushed to the kitchen, grabbed her pastry and mug of mush, and excitedly hurried back. She pulled a chair to the window, sat down, and perked up her ears.

"Everybody criticizes everything nowadays," said Mr. Platzek.

"They used to before, too."

"But nowadays more."

"You think?"

"Or put it this way. Nowadays it's allowed."

"Nowadays all sorts of things are allowed."

"But if I want to give some little shit a slap in the face, that's not allowed."

"No, sir."

"Talking's allowed."

"Yes, sir."

"Nowadays everything's interactive."

"Just about."

"On TV they ask every idiot his opinion."

"You're right about that."

"They invite six idiots and ask them all their opinion."

"Opinion, right. Sometimes not even that."

"And meanwhile nobody thinks at all."

"They didn't used to before, either."

"But at least people used to ponder."

"You think?"

"Well, maybe reflect."

"Reflect, right."

"It wasn't allowed, but they still reflected."

"I don't know if I'd call that reflection."

"Maybe not. But they would imagine different things."

"They do that now, too."

"Nowadays no one imagines anything. All they do is talk."

"That's democracy for you."

"That wasn't allowed before."

"Exactly."

"Nowadays everyone talks and nobody listens."

"No, sir."

"They just all give their opinions."

"Opinions, right."

"You're right. They don't even give their opinions. They just go on and on about things. Every idiot. Before, only some idiots talked."

"That's democracy."

"Everyone else kept their mouth shut."

"What else could they do?"

"You've got to admit, there was something to it."

"Something, yes."

"There were just as many idiots, but most of them kept their mouths shut."

"Hear, hear."

"Is that democratic?"

"Yes."

"That everyone talks and nobody listens?"

"That's right."

"That's a strange sort of democracy."

"We just have to get used to it."

"Maybe it isn't strange. Maybe it's actually true democracy."

"That's entirely possible."

"That everyone talks and nobody listens."

"That's right."

"Listen, I wouldn't want you to think I'm not a democrat, but still."

"Still. On that we agree."

"All everyone does is talk. And yet they've got nothing to say."

"And they don't even know it."

"Don't know what?"

"That they've got nothing to say."

"What else do you expect from a bunch of idiots?"

"Nothing."

"One idiot can't expect another to know they've got nothing to say."

"Of course not."

"There, you see? I can talk and talk and not say a thing, but as soon as I want to light up in the doctor's waiting room or give some brat a beating, that's not allowed."

"No, it's not."

"It was in our day."

"Yes, it was."

"Is that democratic?"

"That it's not allowed?"

"Yeah."

"It depends. If you were that brat . . ."

"Now you sound like they do on TV."

"I hope not."

"I couldn't be that brat, because we had an upbringing."

"You're right about that."

"Nowadays it's all human rights. And no upbringing."

"It's practically a forgotten word."

"Nowadays you can't even smack your own kid."

"You can. You just have to be careful."

"Listen, I lived through the war."

"Those must have been hard times."

"Well, not exactly the war. The mobilization."

"Even so."

"Four nights in the barracks, twenty-four guys in one room."

"That's a lot."

"When they turned out the light, we'd have a contest to see who could let the loudest fart. Originally someone suggested a contest for the smelliest one, but after a couple you couldn't tell, they all merged into one."

"We were all young once."

"But still, I'll tell you one thing. In our day wars made sense."

"All wars make some sense. We just don't know what, exactly."

"Nowadays when someone farts, it's a logical phenomenon."

"Sociological."

"Right. In our day wars were either just or injust. But collectively they made sense. Not like nowadays."

"Times have changed."

"Take the Taliban for example."

"Out of the Taliban into the fire."

"What's that?"

"Nothing. Just a bad joke."

"Oh. But anyway. Tell me, what kind of war was that?"

"You're right. They used to be different."

"And young people nowadays. I mean, it's a joke."

"Always was."

"They don't know how to fart, never mind on command."

"It's hard sometimes."

"But opinions, they've got one of those for everything."

"You know how it is."

"Nowadays everyone knows what they're supposed to think in advance."

"Think, right."

"Or say."

"More like it."

"And no one listens to anyone."

"No one knows how anymore."

"The Jevohah's Witnesses came by to see me the other day."

"Jehovah's."

"And they said nowadays no one listens to anyone anymore. Just like us."

"We're listening to each other."

"But we're saying that nobody listens to anyone."

"That's right."

"And when I told them they could speak their hearts, since I know how to listen, I had an upbringing, not like nowadays . . ."

"Nowadays it's practically a forgotten word."

"Exactly. And when I said that, they said I'd find everything in the Bible and tried to sell me one for two hundred crowns. Said I'd find the way in there. At the bookstore they told me it'd cost three-fifty, at least."

"Everything's more expensive."

"But they didn't want to chat."

"That's rare nowadays."

"Maybe they weren't Jevohah's Witnesses."

"Jehovah's."

"Maybe they were Normans."

"Mormons."

"Right."

"They don't carry the Bible, though. They've got their own."

"There's only one Bible."

"One Holy one. But there are others."

"So they weren't Normans."

"Mormons."

"Right."

"Probably not."

"Maybe they were those Seventh-Day types."

"Adventists."

"Right. Nowadays any idiot's allowed to talk."

"Yes, sir."

"If this is democracy . . ."

"It is."

"Maybe you're right. But what good is it, then?"

"It's democratic."

"But still."

"On that we agree."

"The other day on the radio, the president said that democracy stakes its success on intelligence."

"That isn't dumb."

"No, it isn't. Maybe not. But how many intelligent people do we have?"

"Not many."

"You see?"

"Maybe you're right."

"Nothing against democracy, but I'd rather bet on stupidity."

"It would be easier."

"In our day there wasn't so much talk."

"There was less opportunity."

"Nowadays there's talk everywhere—on the radio, on the television. The only place there isn't any talk is in line. Everyone's quiet there."

"You're right about that."

"Supposedly it's a sign of longevity. Talking. They said so on the radio."

"I hope not."

"I don't believe it. People should keep their mouths shut."

"They'd often be better off."

"In our day, no one talked, women stood in line, and I'm still here."

"You look good."

"Nowadays everyone debates everything. You debate with your children, your wife. In our day . . ."

"Everything used to be simpler."

"People shut their mouths and didn't need to get divorced. Nowadays it's all they do."

"Yes, sir. More and more divorces every day."

"The Taliban banned it."

"They banned a lot of things."

"The other day on TV they said that Muslims and all of those ones with the beards can legally beat their wives if they don't obey. Supposedly it says so in the Koran."

"A beating a day keeps temptation away."

"What's that?"

"Sorry. I was trying to make a joke."

"Oh. Well but supposedly it's literally written there."

"Supposedly."

"That you're allowed to beat your wife."

"Wives."

"That's right. They can have more than one."

"Oh well, different strokes for different folks."

"That's why they wear those beards, too."

"That's required."

"Supposedly they can even kill their daughter if she messes around with someone. Legally. I mean, illegally. That is, they can legally kill them, for messing around illegally."

"Are you sure?"

"That's what they said. Seems excessive to me. A slap or two, all right, but killing your daughter?"

"Oh well, different strokes."

"Although on the other hand, if I had a daughter and she messed around, with a Gypsy, say . . ."

"That's not allowed here."

"Not that I'd kill her, mind you, don't go getting the wrong idea, but she wouldn't be able to sit down for two weeks I'd beat her so bad."

"That's not allowed either."

"Or with the Taliban."

"Especially if she's of age."

"Of age, not of age. A woman's a woman."

"Can't argue with that."

"I should say so. Look at that. See that one there? That's what I'm talking about."

"That Gypsy?"

"There's more and more of them every day."

"They've always been in this neighborhood."

"He's writing something on the wall."

"You're right."

"That wasn't allowed in our day."

"No, sir. But I've got to be going."

"Oh? Well, anyway it was nice to chat."

"You're right. It was very nice."

"Have I seen you around here before? My name's Platzek."

A tomcat by the name of Bugs silently snuggled up to Mrs. Prochazka, rubbing against her shin. Mrs. Prochazka, tense and focused, shrieked in fright. So it was that the closing words escaped her:

"Lebeda. Vilém Lebeda."

16

Indeed, a new piece of graffiti had appeared on the wall: *Ashardi amari buti, you bastards!* Over the next few weeks, the dark-skinned locals stopped in front of it every now and again, amused; to the light-skinned locals the core of the statement remained impenetrable, although they sensed that the comprehensible part, grammatically known as the salutation, was directed at them.

Inspector Lebeda set out on the trail of the unknown epigraphist.

A few years earlier, there had been nothing to suggest that Vilém Lebeda, born 1958, would become a successful criminologist. He was the child of bourgeois, humanistically oriented parents. His mother was a Budapest Jew by origin, the daughter of the owners of a hat-manufacturing firm, who were taken away on the last Hungarian transport to Auschwitz; his father was the firstborn son of a more or less progressive schoolmaster from Nachod. Both his mother and his father were determined to share in the transformation of postwar society, and instilled in their only offspring the extraordinary principle that man is essentially good, and that people should selflessly help one another; and if people did selflessly help one another, the world would soon enter into a new historical era, which would no longer be an era but a category. Later, as it began to dawn on them how poorly they had equipped their child for life, they bitterly regretted it, but it was too late. The young Vilém brought home straight As, helped old people across the street, stood up for the weak, and energetically protested every act of injustice he witnessed. He volunteered with the Red Cross, recycled paper and gave the money to his parents, tutored his less-gifted classmates, went door to door collecting funds for the downtrodden of the world, reasoned with the drunks staggering out of the local pub and the smokers hacking on the benches in the nearby park. Every Saturday afternoon he went to read *Ivanhoe* to the residents of the Institute for the Blind, and he even taught himself sign language, just in case he happened to run into any deaf-mutes. On those rare occasions when he did play a game, he stuck exclusively to those meant to refine and fortify the mind. He was a model son; a model Pioneer; a model Scout; the favorite of sick grandmothers, his teaching staff, and the blind of Prague. In exemplary fashion he walked the dog; brought home wounded birds, run-over pigeons, and semistarved toads; played the violin and the accordion, and, at the age of fifteen, wrote poems about gloomy skies suddenly slashed through by rays of sun sharp as a barber's razor. He was utterly incapable of normal communication: his need to be useful twenty-four hours a day, his unbearably proper speech and eager gaze, full of understanding and love of man, put off every normal person within minutes of meeting him. He was living proof that a person could actually say sentences like "Would you pass me that loaf of bread, friend, I should very much like a bite" or "The darndest thing happened to me yesterday." He had dedicated his life to humanity and the individual, the individual and humanity. Had he been born a few centuries earlier, he might have been Francis of Assisi or Bartholomé de las Casas; in early-seventies Communist Czechoslovakia, he was inevitably taken for an ass.

For that matter, "You officious ass!" was an epithet he was treated to regularly by ungrateful classmates, ungrateful drunks, and ungrateful victims of injustice. Nevertheless, the young Vilém was undeterred: one must be patient with people.

When puberty hit and he began getting pounded by hormones (nature doesn't pick and choose), his curse acquired a new dimension: any potential objects of his sexual desire fled in droves the instant he appeared on the horizon. In vain did he send them impassioned letters; in vain did he try his hand at ballads and alexandrine verse; in vain did he offer to serenade them on the violin—he couldn't have gotten laid if he'd been an egg. In vain did he lower his standards, turning, one by one, to the three ugliest girls in his school: I'm misunderstood, you're misunderstood, let's put our souls together. In vain did he sign up for Communist campouts and ski trips; in vain did he join the Young Conservationists' Club, the Nature Defenders' Society, the Circle of Friends of the Czech Language.

But it wasn't only with young women that Vilém failed to get along. There was also increasing tension in his relationships with adults. Up to then, he had benefited from the fact that he was addressing them from the position of an innocent child; but what passed for charming naïveté, with no ill will, from a child, was viewed as intentional and deliberate provocation from a teenager. If for instance the youthful Vilém addressed someone in a gentle and friendly manner, the person in question inevitably believed the little brat was making fun of him; if he went to the grocery store and asked, "Would you be so kind as to weigh me out three kilograms of those new potatoes?" they tossed him right out the door; if he went into a bookstore and politely inquired, "Excuse me, please. Might I have a glance at this intriguing-looking book?" at best he would be met with an irritated "Listen, kid, don't get smart with me!"

In short, it all began to grate.

Vilém was stunned. To some extent, he had been used to being misunderstood all his life, but he had always assumed that, as the years passed, people would be more willing to listen more closely. He couldn't wait until he grew up. Now, despite his expectations, he was faced with a slippery question: how to live among people and yet still be himself. He sank into a spell of hopelessness and bulimia, putting on a few extra kilos which he would never completely get rid of.

In the end he lost his virginity to his rachitic thirty-eight-year-old neighbor from the fifth floor, whom he delivered groceries to. And they say that charity doesn't pay.

He passed his high school graduation exam no sweat, as well as his university entrance exam. Both of his parents had been thrown out of the Party in '69, but after seven years things had cooled down a bit, especially since his father had been actively working to be re-admitted. I'm doing it for you, he told his wife and son. His wife had stayed at home for the past several years, having been thrown out of not just the Party but also the radio station where she had been employed during the counterrevolution; the future of the family cell, therefore, rested on his father's shoulders. Unfortunately, his wife failed to appreciate his sacrifice; on the contrary, she believed that compromises such as his were unworthy of an honorable man. His parents' arguments multiplied, and when Vilém was in his first year at university his mother went to live with relatives in Hungary and stayed there permanently. She wrote Vilém long letters in which she apologized for not having been able to raise him to live among people who were—well, not necessarily evil, mind you, but came in all sorts—and instructed him to obey his father and follow his advice. Vilém went to Hungary to see his mother regularly, up until her sudden death in '83; by then he was employed as a researcher at the Institute for Controls and Automatics.

He had changed tremendously: no more accosting drunks, no more volunteer rescue work for the Red Cross, he hadn't touched his violin since high school, and had stopped automatically shaking people's hands when he met them. He accepted the fact that people drank alcohol in public; he let his beard grow and began to smoke a pipe; he stopped trying to lure young women to art galleries, instead coming right out and inviting them for coffee. He taught himself to use words like *bike*, *lamebrain*, and *diddly-squat*, and reduced the number of words he used in his sentences by half. When he felt exceptionally good, he even dared to drop a *g* discreetly here and there; once he attempted an *ain't*, but the word got stuck in his throat.

It wasn't that Vilém abandoned his faith in a better world; he simply realized that a better world couldn't be reached by a straight line. It took twists, turns, detours, loops, and backtracking, inconspicuousness and routine, even a certain amount of duplicity and hypocrisy. Having had this realization, Vilém decided to sacrifice some of his secondary ideals.

When in 1991 he came across an announcement of openings in the criminal police, he decided it was a sign of fate, and left his safe and peaceful job at the Institute for Controls and Automatics without regret. He passed the test, as was his wont, no sweat, and stepped into his new position a few weeks later. Over time he established a reputation as a capable if somewhat solitary type. Of his former hobbies, he retained going to the symphony, doing language puzzles in magazines, and composing rhymes for his own pleasure.

Vilém's father, now retired, watched with delight as his son normalized himself. When Vilém turned forty, his father decided that he could speak to him man to man, and told him a secret that he had kept to himself all those years: Vilém had a half brother, the son of a woman by the name of Anna Socher, whom his father had met when he was still single. Years later Vilém's father had run into her on the street, he now married to Vilém's mother, she to a man named Viktor Dyk. One word led to another and word was made deed every Monday and Thursday from 4:30 to 6:00 P.M. But, as the old saying goes, you can't walk 'round a bog without catching cold. A few months later she called him at work in a state of agitation, thus confirming the saying. She urged him to keep the affair to himself and never to get in touch with her again.

Having revealed to his son this hidden episode from his otherwise quiet life, his father caught cold, got the flu, and died.

17

"Anything new? It's about time," said the older man to the younger.

"If you think this is easy . . ."

"All due respect, but that's not my concern. You said two or three months, at most."

"Something came up. Something urgent."

"That's none of my business either. What's new?"

"I might have something. In the Ore Mountains. Near Svahova."

"Yes?"

"Old cabin. One room, stove, bed, table, bench, two flimsy chairs. Dry toilet. Closest water's about a hundred meters away. Supposedly some tramps took it over after the war. Police ran 'em out in the fifties, and in the sixties they went right back. Different ones, of course. Now it's deserted."

"And?"

"Real mess inside. But I found a beat-up suitcase under the bed with some newspapers inside. 1962, -3, -4, and -5."

"And?"

"And this was in there."

The younger man pulled a yellowed magazine from his briefcase.

"Careful or it'll crumble."

The older man slowly flipped through it.

"Page sixteen. Chess column."

The older man turned to page sixteen and raised his eyes in disgust.

"Houska, I said. Vitek Houska. This says Karel Hoska."

"I know. But the year fits: 1963. So does the place: Marienbad. And the month: December."

"Jesus Christ. I said Houska, not Hoska. Vitek, not Karel. And November I said, not December. Besides, do you see any notes?"

"There, underneath. White moves here, black moves there."

"*Handwritten* notes. I said Houska, November, handwritten notes."

"Look, you're the client. But if you think this is easy . . ."

"My dear fellow, there must be a brain in that head of yours somewhere. It's a scientific fact. So use it."

"Just 'cause you paid me doesn't give you the right to insult me . . ."

"I'm not insulting you at all. I'm saying Houska, November, handwritten notes, brain in head, use it."

"I've been in this line of work for thirteen years now. You don't have to lecture me."

"Ignorance is bliss."

"You think you're so smart, don't you?"

"It fouls the air like piss."

"Is that supposed to be about me?"

"Of course not. That's from the Bible."

18

It must have been a bad dream, though it started innocently enough. Dyk Jr. stepped off the train to find himself in an unknown station. He had a vague feeling that he wasn't here by accident, that someone was expecting him, but he wasn't too disturbed that he didn't know who. Eventually he would remember.

It was raining.

Dyk Jr. set his travel bag (or maybe suitcase) down on the drenched concrete of the platform, reached automatically into his pocket for a cigarette and placed it between his lips, shielding it from the wind with his left hand while with the thumb of his right he flicked an imported German lighter engraved with his initials in gold (a gift from his mistress), which, however, didn't make it burn any better. He flicked it again. The cigarette glowed feebly. He took a deep drag and the cigarette shone brighter. As he stowed the lighter back in his pocket, a raindrop fell on his cigarette a couple of millimeters away from the filter. The cigarette buckled limply, the wet paper tore, and the glowing tip dropped to the level of his chin; in a senseless attempt to save what he could, he tried to straighten it out, in one disastrous movement squashing it against his nose and burning his fingers. Dyk Jr. swore to himself and spat out the useless wad in disgust. The train shuddered to a start and inched forward cautiously, as though afraid that it might slip on the wet rails.

He picked up his suitcase (or perhaps travel bag) and strode into the station. For a moment he wondered whether he had the date or the place wrong; no one had gotten off the train except for him and the station hall was empty, apart from a cleaning woman who eyed him with irritation as she splashed a bucket of dirty water underneath his feet. No one was waiting for him in front of the station either. Water ran down his collar onto his neck. What was probably the last bus was just pulling away from a bus stop across the road without a single passenger; it arced toward Dyk Jr., who hesitantly raised his hand. The bus accelerated, seeming to mock him as it drove past through an uninterrupted strip of potholes and puddles in front of the station. Dyk Jr. was about to let loose a string of curses but then thought better of it; the driver was watching him in the rearview mirror and Dyk Jr. had no desire to get his ass kicked in the bargain.

Fine, he'd go on foot then. How far could it be? Six or seven kilometers at most.

Of course he got lost. He ran out of cigarettes, he was hungry, thirsty, his feet hurt, and his bag was getting heavier and heavier. Or suitcase. Woods all around. He was following something that looked like a path. Little by little the rain turned into a storm. The sky was coated with a stroboscopically dripping layer of wet cotton. That isn't bullshit, it's a metaphor.

He was puzzled by the fact that he couldn't hear a sound: no thunder, no rain. Even his own footsteps he could only vaguely hear, muffled, as though coming from far away.

How many kilometers had he come so far? He could barely drag his feet.

In an effort to brighten his forced march, he started trying to think of every phrase he could with the word "foot" in it. Foot it.

Foot the bill. One foot in the grave. On a war footing. To be light-footed, leadfooted. To get cold feet.

He plodded along like that for another half hour, or hour, maybe two. He lost all concept of time. Wear your feet to the bone. Put your foot down. Put your foot in your mouth. When his feet gave out, he switched to his mouth. Put your foot in your mouth. Put your money where your mouth is. Straight from the horse's mouth. Etc. Then hands. Eyes. Ears. Etc.

Hoot owls hooted and screech owls screeched. Because of the rain.

When, lo and behold! A breach in the night! A patch of snowy white amid the trees! Could it be a clearing?

Suddenly, out of nowhere, a cluster of shady figures emerged from under the branches. They seemed to be heading toward him, silently nodding to him as they gradually quickened their pace; some broke into a jerky run. As the figures came closer, he realized they had pigs' heads; except for that, there was nothing else to suggest that it was a bad dream. The pigheads seemed pleased to see him, tossing their snouts and grinning from ear to ear. All of a sudden he realized that it was they he had arranged to meet, and stepped forward to greet them. When they were right on top of him they began snorting loudly; it was the first real sound he had heard since getting off the train. They formed a circle around him. Dyk Jr. got scared. The circle slowly tightened. Their heads were just centimeters away.

Whereupon he awoke. Lying in a strange room on a bench by a stove, shoes under his head and a ragged blanket thrown over him, which whoever it had warmed before, they must've been pretty hot. There was a knock at the door. Dyk Jr. yawned, sat up, tossed off the blanket, shuddered with cold. Yes, some people toss off blankets while others toss off verse; some make blanket statements and some make blanket loans; some folks have knees that knock with cold and others' knuckles knock on doors. So it goes with words, my friends.

19

Viktor Dyk leaned over the parapet of Revolution Bridge, eaves-dropping on Teddy who, seven meters below, was bending the ears of two high school hotties—who'd come with the intention of taking a lazy row downstream while sharing their paltry existential problems with one another—with one historical date after the next. Viktor Dyk listened in with, so to speak, professional interest: in his country, the spewing of dates is a popular variation on the citing of nonexistent sources, which Dyk had chosen as his social strategy years ago. The Czechs believe that anyone who remembers dates can't be totally stupid. The subtle insertion of historical dates into conversation testifies not only to a penetrating intelligence but a vigorous patriotism—twice as desirable at a time when Brussels technocrats were busy thinking up ways to trample the Czech nation under the bureaucratic wafflestomper of Europeanism. In short, the Czechs devote such passion to the memorization of dates that, apart from them, they don't remember anything at all.

If Dyk opted for biblical sources rather than dates, it was for two reasons, which, for that matter, were connected: there was significantly less competition in his chosen field, meaning 1) he could shine all the more brightly, while 2) reducing the risk that anyone might correct him. In addition there was a third, albeit secondary, reason: in high school Dyk had had a classmate—a nerd, brown-noser, star pupil, and tattletale—whom he truly couldn't stand, and who could reel off historical dates like the multiplication table. His name was Karel Krezlar, so the kids in school would taunt him: "Kay Kay goes caca, and he also bugs the shit out of us!"

Karel Krezlar later became a psychologist and wrote popular books on memory and memorization techniques. He even invented a universal mnemonic device consisting of the conversion of consonants to numbers. With the aid of this so-called bridge, whereby numbers were converted into words, a speaker could recall any date at will. (The year 1620, for instance, corresponded to "Fear the night"; the year 1670 to "It was a teacher"; the year 1415 to "Burning log"; and so forth.*) In the late seventies, the method was introduced, on an experimental basis, for instruction to first-year students at three high schools in Brno; it soon became clear, however, that the young learners, failing to grasp the sentences' metaphorical meaning, had more problems remembering the bridges than the years themselves. Most of them spontaneously revised the bridges, based on their own dialectic ("Burning teacher," "Fear the log," "It was at night"), leading them to entirely errant historical conclusions. One such unfortunate became celebrated in professorial circles for an essay in which via Dr. Krezlar's method he arrived at the conclusion that the Battle of White Mountain had taken place in 6702; and since this was a thoughtful student, to whom the absurdity of this statement was immediately obvious, he inserted the brief clarification "before our era."

---

*   1620: defeat of Czech nobles in an uprising against imperial Austria's forces in the Battle of White Mountain. 1670: death of Comenius (Jan Amos Komenský), Czech teacher and scientist, often considered the father of modern education. 1415: Jan Hus, Czech theological reformer, burned at the stake for heresy.

The hotties bailed out relatively quickly, after half a dozen dates.

"We actually just wanted to know how much an hour costs," said the leader of the group—that is, the less hideous of the two.

"Ninety crowns," replied Teddy. "You know how much an hour cost in 1989? Of course not, you were barely even walking then, let alone rowing boats. Five crowns! Five!"

"Okay, thank you." The hotties sidled off.

Dyk stared a while longer at Teddy, who stared a while longer at the hotties. Then he cleared his throat, gathered the phlegm in his mouth, curled his tongue, pursed his lips, and let it fly. A little more oomph and he would have hit his mark. Teddy, hearing the slap of the spit, looked around and lifted his eyes. An old man stood on the bridge, leaning over the parapet. Gazing searchingly into the Vltava's capering waves.

20

"That Kalousek lady is here," said Benedikt Sverak, Vilém Lebeda's direct subordinate.

Sverak's nickname had been Slip for as long as he could remember. According to one version, in his younger years, back in Kladno, while pursuing a fleeing suspect he had slipped on a banana peel tossed on the sidewalk by some negligent citizen and ended up in the hospital. Another version had it that he managed to collar the suspect, but the guy gave him the slip on the way back to the station. Sverak himself, however, denied both accounts, patiently explaining that the reason for his nickname was his skill at slipping out of dangerous situations.

Sverak harbored some bitterness over the fact that he hadn't made it further in his career. He got along with Lebeda for the most part, and being his subordinate was actually fairly easy. But deep down in his soul, he was convinced that Lebeda's job was rightfully his. Trouble is, these days, you gotta have a degree for just about everything. Whenever Lebeda was out, Sverak would go into his office and rummage through his papers, hoping to come across some particularly prickly, impenetrable case that he could secretly crack in his spare time and show all of them, once and for all, that he was more than just an interchangeable paper pusher with outsomu chasa threado fimag I nation. Beginning with his wife and kids.

"Yes? Send her in."

"And also that Ukrainian guy. Kovalenko's his name."

"Tell him to wait. This won't take long."

"If you ask me, there's something kind of suspicious about him."

"How so?"

"Too eager. Nobody even asked him and he just starts explaining what he does, where he works, how many kids he's got. If you ask me, he's an illegal. I wouldn't even be surprised if he's mafia."

"We'll find out soon enough. Now could you send Mrs. Kalousek in?"

"Kalousek!" Sverak yelled down the hall, and marched out of the room.

A plain-looking woman of about forty poked her head in the door.

"Mrs. Kalousek?" Lebeda inquired affably.

"Kalous," the woman said inaudibly.

"Pardon me?"

"Kalous. No *ek*. *Kay* at the beginning. No *ek* at the end," she said more audibly.

When she was single, Mrs. Kalousek's name had been Kalous. Thus her change in marital state had given her the status of a diminutive, which she bore devotedly if resentfully—until, after seven years of marriage, she got divorced and went back to her maiden name. But it drove her friends out of their minds.

"Oh, I'm sorry," said Lebeda. He stood politely, closed the door behind Mrs. Kalous, and slid a chair toward her.

"Please, have a seat."

Mrs. Kalous gingerly had a seat.

"I've got nothing to be guilty about."

"Pardon me?"

"I said I've got nothing to be guilty about. I live alone with my son. People don't like it, but he goes to school regularly and studies hard. Someone must've said something nasty about us."

"No one did any such thing, Mrs. Kalous. I wanted to meet with you because of the events in your building. You know, those two fires."

"All the papers ever write about is human rights, but they don't like it."

"Pardon me?"

"People. They don't like it."

"Yes, I see. But if you don't mind, I'd like to ask about the fires."

"I know nothing about it."

"Pardon me?"

"I don't know a thing. The firemen came. The building was full of smoke."

"You live on the second floor, is that right?"

"One of them was very nice. Handsome. And brave, with an ax."

"Pardon me?"

"An ax. I don't know anything else. Really, you've got to believe me."

"Oh, I do, Mrs. Kalous, don't worry. But I wanted to ask if you've run into anyone strange in the building, a man, a woman, downstairs, upstairs, anywhere. Maybe they had the wrong address, or came to visit someone—anyone at all who you've never seen before."

"Just Mr. Alexi. But I run into him almost every day. He's Ukrainian. Polite, though. Says hello, sometimes twice, even—when I answer and he doesn't hear—and he thinks *I'm* the one who can't hear. My hearing's fine. But there's a lot of them here. Him, his brother, his wife, and two daughters. In two rooms."

"Yes, but anyone you don't know?"

"Not counting the entryway."

"Who?"

"The entryway. That doesn't count."

"I see. Thank you for your trouble, Mrs. Kalous."

"That's all?" she said, in a tone both relieved and disappointed.

"That's all."

21

Walking to the other bank (coming back he took the tram: traveling via public transportation between five and six in the evening was one of the funnest things that he treated himself to regularly), Dyk recalled another idiot he used to know, the husband of a colleague of his whose horns he had polished for two or three years. On an office retreat he once spent an entire week with him.

"Naiman, architect."

And I'm an archangel, moron.

"Dyk."

"Ah, so you're the infamous Mr. Dyk."

Clever.

"Yeh."

"You work with my wife, right?"

Why, you might even say I work closely with her.

"That's right."

"Pleased to meet you."

Wish I could say the same.

"Likewise."

Naiman was such a perfect example of Czech idiocy that he could have been an exhibit at the World's Fair: jovial, cautious, adequately traditional, adequately uneducated, haughty, smug, and aggressive. Overly fond of *debating*, which in Czechia is understood to mean a social exercise whose object is to crush some other moron trying to state his opinion. Only by acquitting himself of this societal obligation is a Czech considered intelligent: Czech intelligence springs from the dark depths into which one semi-idiot hurls another. *Arguing*, then, amounts to the rejection of anything uttered by anyone else as a matter of principle—they're not going to top *me*—while *having an opinion* means regarding the ooze in your own head as the most precious thing in the world.

Naiman excelled at *debates*, *arguments*, and *having opinions*, as a result of which he enjoyed the respect and esteem of his fellow citizens: for to express one's idiocy with all the authority presumed by such behavior is the highest ambition for Czechs, falling immediately after the organization of fruitful collaboration with the powers that be, and the construction of rock gardens.

In 1968, Naiman emigrated to France—he left his wife at home, which very much appealed to Dyk, at least until she started to talk about divorce—with a patriotic resolution to show the great wide world outside how incredible Czechs really are. When after four or five months he discovered how stupid and dense the great wide world was, he decided it was time to return to his homeland, and did. Naiman took away two incontrovertible truths from his cosmopolitan experience: the world is full of idiots, and a Czech is too refined and contemplative a creature to be able to live a full life anyplace else but among his own. To Dyk's great relief, Naiman took back his increasingly excitable wife, bought a semi-broken-down cottage in the middle of the woods, covered it with a thatched roof, put a granite basin under the water pump, and became a tireless propagator of south Bohemian folk architecture; he published several books crawling with casings, collar beams, eaves plates, yealms, stelches, and flanking bays. Say what you will: the world is the world, but thatching is thatching.

Dyk ran into Naiman again, years later, in the waiting room of one Dr. Petranek—a testicologist who, under the pretense of preventing testicular atrophy, measured men's balls and prescribed vitamins. Naiman went on for forty-five minutes about folk architecture and the shallowness of the Western world, interlacing his lecture with quips and puns about testicles, balls, ballrooms, and nuts: in the Czech lands, even intellectuals know how to have a good laugh.

Naiman died as stupidly as he lived. One day he decided to get a new washing machine for the cottage. But what to do with the old one? He loaded it into his car, drove into the forest, and rolled the machine to the top of a hill, intending to push it into a gorge; one garbage dump more or less, the Czech woods had survived worse. But no matter how hard he leaned into the thing, it wouldn't budge, so, taking a few steps back, he sprinted forward, spinning around and throwing his haunches into it; the washer sailed into the gorge and Naiman along with it. Some nosy hiker discovered the body five days later, and the *South Bohemian Tribune* ran a brief obituary headlined "Expert Meets Tragic Death."

Dyk gave a creaky laugh. Memories are the balm of old age.

Through the sweat, spite, and exhaust fumes, the crowd of passengers waiting at the tram stop quivered in the sun. Standing on the concrete island surrounded by traffic, they looked like an ark of castaways who hadn't been able to make up their minds which shore they wanted to land on.

Dyk breezily pushed through the crowd, chuckling to himself as he whacked his cane through the thicket of ankles and calves.

A few bystanders turned their heads in irritation. Registering their hostile looks, Dyk drew a deep breath and belched loudly. He knew from experience it would taint the air around him for a meter and a half at least.

22

"Kovalenko!" Sverak announced. "And meantime some other guy came in."

"Hroznata."

"Yeah, that's him. And then there's the owner of the Massage Center, but I sent him to Hybler."

"What's bothering him?"

"His front window got sprayed. Third time this month. They painted, begging your pardon, dicks all over the glass. So I sent him to Hybler."

"You did right. Send Mr. Kovalenko in."

"By the way, that Naiman lady didn't show. Should I call her up and chew her out?"

"Not yet, thanks."

Mr. Kovalenko entered. Big nose, fancy mustache, rat's chin, pig lips. Lyrical and overrespectful. He had caught a nasmork the night before the fire and was laid up in bed with a runny nose, swallowed half a kilo of pills, head like a blown-up galosh, he heard nothing, saw nothing, felt nichevo. Could one of his tenants have started the fire? No, he refused to believe it, and as a foreigner who had come to this hospitable country to find work, and who aspired to be a loyal subject of his fellow Slavic narod, small in expanse yet large in soul, it wasn't his place to pass judgment. His neighbors were cheerful and hospitable, and he always greeted them courteously. In Mr. Kovalenko's opinion, each and every one of his fellow grazhdanins was the very embodiment of cheerfulness and hospitality, utterly incapable of conceiving any objectionable act, not to mention one punishable by law, let alone committing it. In fact, Czechs were such kindhearted ludyi there were times when it made Mr. Kovalenko's head spin. By the way, if the chief komisar might kindly put in a word with his koleg from the Foreigners' Police . . .

"God bless President," concluded Mr. Kovalenko, crossing himself.

Meanwhile, Sverak was racking his brains trying to figure out why Lebeda was dragging these people into his office instead of sending someone out to talk to them. He shared his bewilderment with his colleague Lieutenant Valach, but Valach didn't understand it any more than Sverak did.

Lebeda had his reasons, though, and his technique was deliberate. This way, he thought, word would get out, and they might prevent a third fire. Lebeda was a methodical soul and a conscientious policeman.

23

The shoebox was clearly new and, on top of that, plastered with all sorts of logos, but its contents were all from the fifties and sixties of last century: one hiking map; one wedding announcement; an embryonic stamp collection in the form of an A6 envelope with some twenty Czech, Slovak, and Hungarian specimens; a green school notebook (subject, name, school, grade); and some pages torn from a scratch pad with a drawing of the sun over a wooded hill and the words "We are of one blood, you and I!" Besides the stamps and papers, the box also contained a plush teddy bear with a dull-witted expression and the name TEDDY on its chest, and a scrap torn from a newspaper with a chess diagram:

Black to move wins.

Viktor Dyk knew the solution by heart: 1. . . . Rgh8 2. Bf3 Qxg4 3. Bg2 Nxg2 4. Qxg2 Rh1+ 5. Qxh1 Rxh1+ 6. Kxh1 Qh3+ 7. Kg1 Qh2+ 8. Kf1 f3 etc.

Or 3. Qe2 Qh3 and White could go take a flying leap.

At least according to the chess editor, who was winner and loser alike.

But there was something they'd overlooked: 3. Rxe3 Qxf3 4. Ng5+ fxg5 5. Rxe7 Kxe7 6. Qg7+ Kd8 7. Qc7+ Ke8 8. Re1+ Qe3 9. Rxe3+ and Black could go take a flying leap.

Or not?

Dyk was beginning to tire of the whole affair. And that idiot had it all wrong. Except for the cabin. Which was the main thing. I know the spot and I can save myself some fees.

Dyk returned the scrap to the box, took out the teddy bear, laid it on its back; it made a grrring. He set aside the teddy bear and reached for the notebook. Written on the cover in a schoolchild's hand was *Alone Among The Utahs: A Novel Of The Wild West*.

The novel was written alternately in pencil and pen, furnished with many illustrations, and preceded by "A Word Of Introduction From The Author":

"I wrote this book for children ages ten and up. Even in my youth I was drawn by a longing for adventure. Which is the reason why I decided to write this book. I know that, now, many children are sitting over this book absorbed in adventure. But, I also wrote this book for adults. My aim is for it to remind them of their youthful longings. I hope you enjoy this book and novel."

At any rate Dyk enjoyed it. He spent the rest of the evening reading.

24

Readers! Does our story seem rambling? Do you have the feeling that the plot is at a standstill? That, generally speaking, nothing much is going on in the book you now hold in your hands? Do not despair: Either the author's a fool or you are; the odds are even. Others have died and so shall we, we'll die, oy vey, alack, alas! Who on earth knows how on earth it will turn out! Sometimes a person gets tangled up in his own life without realizing it; and the same is true of characters in novels.

You ask, How will it all end? But that, dear readers, we cannot reveal. We began this story with no clear aim or preconceived idea. How it will turn out, we do not know; whether it will turn out, we haven't a clue. We're in the same boat as you, or almost, since at this moment, as you read our book, our work is done; the book is out, you bought it, invested part of your earnings in the hope that it would pay off in the form of spiritual dividends. We don't mean to be impolite, we have no intention of committing cheap provocations, and yet, and yet, and yet: what do we care? We've assumed the majority of responsibility; now it's up to you to patiently bear *your* share.

25

The monastery in Osek was built at the very start of the thirteenth century. Seven hundred and fifty years later, an internment center for monks was established in its place, whose raison d'être ended with the inauguration of a new historical era of joyful and creative ferment. A monk, glum and scowling, was as useful to this new age as shins to a fish.

Guarding the friars wasn't exactly hard labor, and the twelve armed men recruited for this purpose spent most of their days being bored. To pass the time they held shooting contests, taking aim at the delirious figures of Gothic and Baroque paintings, statues of various saints, and grotesque waterspouts shaped like frogs, dogs, and other more or less recognizable animals. At night they built a fire—out in the garden, weather permitting; inside the church, when it was inclement—and roasted sausages. Lighting the fire with books from the convent library, they fed it with household furniture. Feasting on sausages and sipping bottled beer, they had long, serious talks about the new era, looking forward to leaving behind their dull monastery assignment in favor of shooting saboteurs on the nearby border. At night they dreamed of moving targets and World War III. Meanwhile the monks trudged the corridors, mumbling unintelligible sayings and dying off, one by one; within three years their numbers had dropped to two hundred.

After another ten years, part of the monastery was made accessible to the public. After another ten years, the monastery had become so dilapidated that the accessible part was declared inaccessible. After another fifteen years, the monastery was returned to the Cistercians. After another fifteen years, part of the monastery was once again made accessible to the public.

An unknown man—crooked teeth, rabbity overbite—walked down the corridor past the refectory, now housing a dozen homeless men who had taken shelter in the monastery. He gave a friendly wave to one.

He walked out to the garden, descended a gentle slope to the town square, and headed for his car. He had a hundred kilometers of hazardous road ahead of him.

A voice blared from his pocket.

"Yes?" he said into the device.

"It's me," rasped the voice. "Havlik."

"Uh-huh. What's up?"

"He goes to Chomutov regularly. Stays two or three days. Private apartment. 4 Palacky Street. But listen, we still have a deal, right?"

"You can count on me."

"I just want to make sure you don't screw me on this. I get hired by all sorts, you know. Some people—"

"I know. Everything's A-OK."

"Great."

26

Benedikt Sverak brought in Mr. Hroznata.

"Please, have a seat," said Lebeda.

Hroznata had a seat.

"So, did he confess?"

"Who? To what?"

"Look, you can level with me. The Ukrainian. Kovalenko. He set the place on fire so they'd put him up in a hotel. Him and his brother and that harem of theirs."

"What makes you think that?"

"Come on, I told you. You can level with me. I wasn't born yesterday."

"No?"

"He acts like Mr. Nice Guy, bowing and scraping and kissing your you-know-what. And meanwhile he's working under the table. Need anything fixed, Mr. Hroznata? Can I paint something? Wash your windows? Then he makes off with the down payment. Or worse. Let him in your apartment and two weeks later you're cleaned out. Perpetrators unknown. What a coincidence."

"Concerning the fire, Mr. Hroznata. Can you tell me anything else?"

"I was at the pub with my buddies, if that's what you want to know. But my wife was home. She doesn't go out in public much.

She doesn't go anywhere, really. And she heard them laughing. The Ukrainian women. Two floors down. You think that's normal? To hear them from two floors down?"

"Yes, interesting. You didn't happen to run into anyone else in the building? When you were on your way out to the pub?"

"Just those grandads who meet down there in that club of theirs. I tell you, whatever they do down there, it's a mystery to me. One time the head grandad tried to get me to join. As if I needed that. Are you getting all this down? What I'm telling you here?"

"This isn't an interrogation, Mr. Hroznata. I just wanted to meet you."

"Yeah well, now we've met. But are you, you know, gonna remember all this?"

"The general outlines, yes. That's enough for me for now."

Mr. Hroznata's face clouded over with disappointment. The spoken word is like a fart: it draws attention for an instant, but then immediately dissolves into the ether; whereas the written word is a bequest to future generations. What Mr. Hroznata didn't realize was that we had taken charge of the work that he expected from Inspector Lebeda, thereby assuring him of far greater renown than he could ever have hoped for from even the most lively written police report.

"I hope your wife has recovered," Lebeda resumed. "Two fires in such a short time."

"She doesn't go out much," said Hroznata.

27

It must have been a bad dream, though it started innocently enough. Dyk Jr. tossed away his cigarette and pressed the buzzer.

Inside, excited voices of various pitch and tone rang out—Good God! Dyk Jr. thought. Next thing he knew, the door swung wide and six or seven unfamiliar laughing faces crowded into the frame.

"Good evening . . . Hello . . ." said Dyk Jr. "I'm . . ."

"Don't say it! Don't say it!"

"Slowpoke!" called out a pinkish female mug on the left.

Slowpoke had been Dyk Jr.'s nickname in high school.

"It's Slowpoke!" "Slowpoke!" "Slowpoke came!" the faces cried, each one more excited than the next. With that, they stood out of the way and Dyk Jr. stepped into a passageway roaring with laughter, the end of which was crowded with still other figures, more loosely arranged.

"You know how I recognized you?" a voice behind him squealed.

Another distantly familiar mug approached him, gave him a slap on the back, and pulled him into the next room. There was a sound of clinking bottles and glasses, and a flurry of grunts, like a congress of hedgehogs in session.

So how was he doing? Good, and him? Not bad, not bad, a little sad, ha-ha, and him? Still up to the same old tricks? Yes, I guess you could say so. What does he mean, he guesses? Troubles, huh? No, he knows how it is, he doesn't have to tell him, upon the journey of our life, midway, ha-ha, yeh-yeh, and how 'bout kids, kids nyet? Kids nyet, how 'bout a wife? Wife nyet? Wife nyet, man, some guys have got all the luck, ha-ha! So, how 'bout they trade numbers, go for a beer and catch up, what's new and how're things, yeah, that'd be great, right? Right? Reminisce about old times, gettin' laid left and right, sprightly young things, pining youths, fantastical nights, gallant days, kids nyet, wife nyet, man, some guys have got all the luck, yeah, that'd be great, right? What do you mean, phone nyet? Phone nyet, how 'bout a cell? Cell nyet too, how 'bout at work? Nyet phone at work too, good grief! Work nyet? Work nyet too, man, some guys have got all the luck!

"Slowpoke!"

Some dolled-up old bag with massive udders weaved through the crowd toward him from the other side of the room. One hand waving feverishly, the other holding a half-eaten piece of vanilla cake with almonds.

"Slowpoke! Hello there! C'mere and give me a kiss!"

Jiggling her tits, she pressed against him thirstily, attaching herself to his lips, sticking out her tongue, and stuffing it in his mouth. Dyk Jr. felt sick.

Whereupon he awoke. Lying on a bench in an empty train compartment, folded coat under his head, sweat streaming off his forehead, and the aftertaste of rancid almonds in his mouth. The train began to brake. Dyk Jr. looked out the window. He'd nearly slept through his stop.

28

"Viktor Jary?" said the bookseller. "Never heard of him."

"It came out around '74 or '75," said Lebeda.

"I got some Czech prose in day before yesterday. Estate. Literary critic. Six hundred volumes at five crowns apiece. I sell a hundred for fifty, I make two thousand. But they aren't unpacked yet."

"I can stop in next week."

"How about some poetry?"

"Maybe next time."

The bookseller reached for a stack of books on the counter and handed Lebeda a slim volume in pastel brown. The author was Jan Chulik and the title was *In a Whirl of Autumn Leaves*.

"One crown fifty," said the bookseller. "And I can write you a dedication, too. Chulik, that's me."

"Really?" said Lebeda politely. "Then I'll definitely take it."

"Hold on," said the bookseller, yanking it out of Lebeda's hand. "So you're not buying a pig in a poke."

He flipped to a certain page, raised the hand holding the book to chest level, leaned the other against the counter, and cleared his throat.

"In the deep of a wood bluish-black laments a doe . . ."

Chulik interrupted himself. "I like tradition, you know. Modern poetry's not for me."

"I understand," said Lebeda.

Chulik cleared his throat.

> *"In the deep of a wood bluish-black laments a doe,*
> *sensing that, alas, her final hour is at hand.*
> *From the silken fields a partridge warbles long and low,*
> *the scent of bacon wafts from a cottage 'cross the land.*
>
> *Springs a poison mushroom from the rampant undergrowth,*
> *liken to the love which I can give to you no more.*
> *Amassed have I too many a fault and failing both,*
> *I listen to the wind at the crossroads howl and roar.*
>
> *Amid the clearing I hear a buck, and woe to him—"*

"I'll take two," said Lebeda.

"The second one's free," chortled Chulik. "Who is this for?"

"Vilém Lebeda. The other one you can just sign."

"To my dear friend Vilém Lebeda, I respectfully dedicate this fistful of autumn verse," said Chulik aloud as he wrote. "Jan Chulik. Hold on. Let me get you a bag."

Lebeda laid one crown fifty on the counter.

"Thank you very much," he said. "And if you have a chance to look around for that Viktor Jary . . ."

"I'll unpack them today," said Chulik. "If it's not there, I'll call around. We'll dig it up somewhere, don't worry."

"That's very kind of you."

"*Life Gone By*, you said?"

"To come. *Life to Come.*"

"Ah yes. Try back tomorrow."

"I'd be delighted."

"So long for now. Tomorrow you can tell me how you liked it."

"I'd be delighted."

29

The new day announced itself every bit as senselessly as those that came before. Dyk, an adherent of rising late, sat in the kitchen sipping coffee, his momentarily toothless mouth gumming a roll with marmalade, reading the classified ads. He flipped past jobs, apartments, and automobiles, and plunged into the personals. The three columns on the left were for women (Female seeks male), the ones on the right for men (Male seeks female). The ads themselves were each preceded by a title in capital letters, turning them into miniature stories. AUTUMN APPROACHES. *Seeking a man with a settled past who doesn't want to be alone.* Dyk, although unschooled in the communication sciences, judged the author to be a woman of about forty—if she were older, it wouldn't occur to her to mention a settled past, let alone to demand it of others—most likely divorced, with two teens at home. Don't want to be alone? Ho-ho! There's a whole team of us! SEEKING MR. RIGHT. *Divorced* (again) *with lovely son* (again), *seeking sincere and responsible partner with sense of humor.* A sense of humor was one of the most common requirements, presumably because it was believed to be the best defense against disillusion. Got a sense of humor? I'm dumb, fat, and sloppy, hope you got the hots! *Likable* and *easygoing* were also in demand—in other words the kind of man who isn't easily thrown. WILL I FIND YOU? *Single mom with small boy seeking kind, easygoing man who puts family first.* No fucking here, but you'll bust your ass to support some other guy's kid! Some titles rhymed: SUMMER BREEZE, WINTER SKIS; others were like echoes of Dyk's youth: SEEKING MAN WITH PICKAX. But the present-day was present as well: BUSINESS-MINDED? *Seeking solvent man. I'm a full-figured* (ho!) *brunette with well-rounded interests in sports and culture* (heh-heh!) *and a general knowledge of economics and law* (ha-ha!). *I know how to support both in business and the rest of life, and how to hold you* (I certainly hope so) *and caress your soul* (huh-huh!) *in hard times.* (And what about easy times? Bitch!) *Prague or Pilsen.* Or how about eat shit and die.

Some women tried to attract men by referring to what they *loved*: humor, dancing, nature, children. They all had *well-rounded interests*, that is to say, generally two (culture and sports, culture and travel, children and culture, family and travel, children and family). Some sought a man *not only* for something (good times, relaxing times, sunny days), but also for something else, although without stating what that something actually was. The man with the pickax was an exception; most of the women wanted *post-HS or HS*, citing their own education (*HS or post-HS*) or *well-rounded interests* (culture, sports, travel, family, children). None of them were attractive, but plenty of them had *been told they were attractive*, or were *of athletic build* (great, a discus thrower . . .). COME INTO MY VOICE MAIL, as one ad was headed, struck Dyk as near pornographic.

The doorbell rang. Dyk swept the crumbs off his pajamas, put in his dentures, and went to answer the door. Standing in the hallway was a squarely built man with an affable smile.

"Viktor Dyk? I'm sorry to bother you. Inspector Lebeda, Vilém Lebeda. I was hoping to have a word with you."

"Me? What did I do this time?"

This seemingly bland question was, for someone of Dyk's generation, neither bland nor seemingly. Twenty or thirty years ago, that sort of sarcasm would have resulted in a thorough police hazing, and, with a little bad luck, a slap or two or a knocked-out tooth. On the other hand, in those days it would have been unthinkable for a cop to introduce himself and apologize for interrupting. Dyk had no way of knowing that this change wasn't due to the new era, but to Inspector Lebeda's personality; although to be thorough we should note that, under the last regime, Inspector Lebeda's personality most likely would have hampered him from rising to the position of security corps officer and chief inspector in the first place.

"Nothing, Mr. Dyk. At least, not that we're aware of." This use of the plural was a standard recommendation of police psychologists. The suspect, given to understand from this response that he was dealing with a nationwide institution, thoroughly modern and well equipped, was then supposed to falter and commit some sort of slip-up. For instance he might shout "It wasn't me!"—thereby giving the investigator an opening to follow that up with: "So who was it, then?"

"It wasn't me," said Dyk, savoring the audacity of his reply.

"We aren't accusing you of anything," replied Lebeda, disregarding the dictates of police psychology. For him, the use of the plural was a way to indicate that his statement was merely a sop to professional praxis; he meant nothing personal by it. "On the contrary, it's an honor to meet you." This transition from plural to singular was in accord with Western humanist tradition, thereby deepening the two men's thus far only superficial relationship through implicit reference to the universality of the individual. "I've always had great respect for writers."

Dyk softened a little, in spite of the fact that he knew better than anyone what crap his writing was. Not that people seemed to care. After the television show revealing that Viktor Jary and Viktor Dyk were one and the same, his neighbors began to greet him with more respect, and when the baker discovered that she was in the presence of a customer whose face had appeared on the small screen, she stopped trying to palm off day-old bread on him. His general practitioner even prescribed him two brand-new pills.

"They often awaken feelings in us we weren't aware of," Lebeda went on.

Dyk decided to interpret the remark positively.

"Those just awakening see farther than the wakeful."

"I wouldn't have thought of that."

"Matthew 11:8."

"Really?"

"Eight or ten."

"My dear Mr. Dyk, I'm delighted that chance has allowed me to meet such an educated man. Might I be so bold as to ask for a moment of your time? I could invite you to my office for coffee, or to a restaurant for lunch. If you don't object, actually I'd prefer lunch."

"But of course. Just because Europe takes us for beggars, doesn't mean we can't enjoy a civil, courteous lunch together."

"I couldn't have put it better myself. Do you know that new restaurant on Hussite Street? I believe it used to be called The Sycamore? Tomorrow around noon?"

"It will be my pleasure."

30

"So why did you really come to Prague?" asked Benedikt Sverak.

"Like I said, I had an appointment with Professor Pelan."

"That's your fiancé?"

"Of course not, he's a professor."

"So he can't be your fiancé?"

"Obviously. I mean, not obviously, that's not what I mean. I'm just saying—he's a professor at the Academy."

"I see."

"Of Fine Arts."

"Married?"

"Yes."

"So he's your lover."

"No, not my lover." (Miss Reis's face turned red.) "I already told you, he's a professor."

"Fine, whatever you say. So, you were on your way to an appointment with Professor Penal."

"Pelan."

"Pelan. Where at?"

"The Academy, like I told you."

"You took the tram from the station?"

"Yes. I missed my stop, then I got mixed up, and by that point I was late and I was totally soaked in sweat."

"Just a minute. You said the culprit assaulted you on Puklich Street."

"Right. By the alley."

"You say you were in a rush. So what were you doing on Puklich Street?"

"I told you. I was rushing to make my appointment."

"You already said that. I'm asking what you were doing on Puklich Street."

"That's where I got jumped."

"You already said that too. But for him to be able to jump you, you must have followed him there."

"I didn't follow anyone. I was on my way to an appointment with Professor Pelan. And he jumped out of the alley."

"The professor?"

"No! The culprit!"

"The tram stops on Soviet Heroes. Roosevelt, I mean. So how did you end up on Puklich?"

"I took that other street. Hollar, I think."

"You think? Or you're sure?"

"I'm sure I took some other street to get to Puklich. I think it was called Hollar."

"And you rode the tram."

"That's what I said."

"And you claim you had an appointment with Professor Penal at the Academy."

"Pelan. Yes. What's wrong with that? My mom's friend was a witness at his sister's wedding."

"I'm not saying there's anything wrong with it. After all, this isn't a hundred years ago, right? Now, you claim you had an appointment with the professor. At the Academy."

"Yes. Of Fine Arts."

"So what were you doing on Puklich Street?"

"What do you mean, what was I doing? Why do you keep asking what I was doing there? That's where I got jumped."

"Know what? Let's take it again from the beginning. What time did you get to Prague?"

31

Vilém Lebeda strolled home. As was his habit, he had gotten off the tram three stops before his own so he could go the rest of the way on foot. This was his way of putting the office out of his mind; occasionally it worked. Once home, he would eat dinner, change into his nightclothes, brew some mint tea, and put on a divertimento. Or a string quartet. Ever since his father's death he had lived in their three-room apartment alone.

The dopey faces of the politicians on the posters hanging up around town reminded him of the upcoming elections. *The right people in the right places.* Lebeda voted regularly, believing the act of voting to be an inseparable part of full-fledged citizenship. But the choice grew harder year by year, the dopey faces increasingly dopey and Lebeda's weariness increasingly wearying. *We chose you, you choose us.* Unlike a growing number of his fellow citizens, Lebeda believed in the democratic system, however imperfect it was. But the faith in the future he had felt ten years ago had left him. Mr. Platzek was right in at least one respect: human idiocy is the one thing on earth that offers us some idea of infinity.

And if anyone were to ask Lebeda now—frankly; flat out; without any fuss, fooling around, or beating around the bush, as is the Czech nation's nature—"Are you *really* a democrat?" he wouldn't be able to answer without hesitation. *Vote with your heart* and *your head.*

Actually, he could answer three ways. The first was the most practical, being utterly unconvincing: "Do I look like a Communist?" The most practical because every Czech looks like a Communist; and for the same reason unconvincing. The second, less practical but more political option consisted of a counterattack: "Are *you*?" Less practical because it could cause the exchange to drag on; more political since the respondent thus made it clear that when it came to basic values he was prepared to engage in conflict, even as he implied that he and his questioner shared something in common. The third option was less potent socially but intellectually more impressive: "First we'd have to define what we mean by 'democracy.'"

The land for the people. Better government for a better life. Join us against corruption.

The question would have been awkward for Lebeda regardless. As a humanist he believed—or, to be more precise, trusted—in the nobility of the soul. Yet squaring the nobility of the soul with the notion of democracy is impossible: in democracy it's the people who rule, not the person, and the people don't believe in nobility any more than they do in the soul.

The people profess other values.

Another reason to hesitate in giving a response was that he set at least as much store by order and social conventions as he did by individual freedom. In fact, had he been able to suppress all his prejudices and ignore his upbringing, he probably would have declared himself a royalist. To be sure, enlightened monarchy is a rare commodity, but it has existed a few times before, while no one has ever seen an enlightened democracy. The res publica is a fine idea, if only there were a way to take the people out of it. *Change with us.*

Vilém Lebeda was ashamed of himself. Thinking like that. He, a former Pioneer, an erstwhile Scout, and to this day a redoubtable philanthropist. Sighing, he took his pipe from his mouth and scratched his head with the stem. Tonight he would go to bed early. Tomorrow he had to be in shape: a conversation with Mr. Dyk awaited him.

32

It must have been a bad dream, though it started innocently enough. The light, murky and reluctant, suggested that day had not yet fully dawned. Still, even at this early hour, some little nosewipe sat on the curb across from the bus stop with a rebellious kitten in his lap, trying to poke out its eye with a bit of twig. Silently Dyk Jr. bent down, picked up a stone, and heaved it at him. The nosewipe yelped and jumped up, dropping the kitten. "You prick!" he shouted. Blood ran down his forehead. Nearby, a dog began to bark. Dyk Jr. bent down for another stone. The nosewipe ran for it. More dogs joined in, a window shutter clapped open.

Dyk Jr. walked through the village, heading toward the cemetery. The barking of dogs slowly dwindled. Dyk Jr. realized he had left his suitcase on the bus. Or bag.

He stopped uncertainly.

Groped in his pocket, counting how many cigarettes he had left. Six. Pick up sticks. Sticks and stones may break my bones. Enough to last him two hours. At most. Maybe he should just give it up and wait for the bus back to Chomutov?

Well, as long as I'm here.

He opened the cemetery gate. Seventeen or eighteen graves. The three oldest dated from the start of the nineteenth century. Matyas Bartoch, draftsman for the Royal and Imperial district office; Meine Werteste Wilhelma Klein, wife of the master tailor in Hradek; and

Alessandro Catalano, former Kaiserlicher Antekammerthürhüter to the court in Vienna. Cemetery cosmopolitanism as a testimonial to more or less unsettled lives.

Most of the graves were younger by fifty to a hundred years; the stone crosses gradually crowded out by brass ones, marble beginning to make its way into the tombstones. The number of Czech names decreased, but he who laughs last, and all that: the latest arrival was Jan Ryba * 5. 1. 1932, † 16. 6. 1939.

Adjoining the east wall was a row of twelve tombs, put in by the local vicar Dietrich Dietmar in the 1880s; he had handcarved each one with a rhymed epigram relating to this or that grave, then outfitted each with an iron cross with the corresponding number.

1. For a mother sore good:
Here sleeps in the Lord a mother to her children sore good,
She sought to bring them joy whene'er and howe'er she could.

5. For a lazar:
In misery, woe, and hardship a human life abounds,
For dancing and delight it offers precious little grounds.

30. For a woman with terrible illness:
Her face with scabbing almost wholly overlaid,
'Til death did bring end to her woe and to her life put paid.

38. For every mortal:
With every breath we toward death rush,
Of health, strength, vigor, soon nary a blush.

Dyk Jr. picked his way through the graves. The numbered ones he could ignore; Dietmar the vicar had passed away in 1901, and no one had had the nerve to continue the work he'd begun. Dietmar, however, having foreseen the situation, had chiseled his own epitaph into the last tomb:

> *He who has served Verse in life shall find here peace and order,*
> *Let the world rage and storm, he lies safe beyond its border.*

Dyk Jr. was roughly halfway through his search when he heard the sound of agitated voices at the gate. The nosewipe, forehead bandaged, was accompanied by two men—parent and grandparent, to judge from their appearance; the older gripped a rifle, the younger one a shovel. "That's him!" the nosewipe shrieked. "Hey you, c'mere! Hey, shithead!" his daddy bellowed, brandishing the shovel.

His grandfather silently, steadily took aim.

Dyk Jr. was scared. The last time he'd had his ass kicked was at age seventeen, by some members of the working class waiting for the first morning tram in an outlying district of Prague; he had been on his way home from a party with his pal, one Michal Stavarich, who came up with the bright idea of addressing the dreary figures:

"Yeah, you jerks, you go right ahead and bust your butts while we go to school for you!"

A brief chase ensued. They sobered up pretty quick; it took some doing to shake their pursuers. They finally came to a breathless stop, thinking it was over, when suddenly a lunch pail came sailing around the corner and slammed into the back of Dyk Jr.'s neck. He caught the next blow from the pavement, Stavarich swore out loud and took off, the workers closed in and stomped Dyk Jr. to a pulp.

"I said, c'mere!"

Shovel man came up the middle of the graveyard, the gunman curving around in tow. The nosewipe stood in the gateway, bouncing up and down angrily. Dyk Jr. made a break for the opposite wall. Either he'd try to sprint down the side lane and make a beeline back to the gate while shovel man was busy hurdling tombstones, or he'd have to jump the wall. Either way, there wasn't much time to decide.

"Stop! You hear?"

Over the wall would be safer.

"Shoot! What're you waitin' for?"

Dyk Jr. panicked.

"Stop or I'll shoot!"

Building up speed, he was just about to vault the wall when a shot rang out behind him.

That woke him up. He was lying on a bench in an empty train station waiting room, travel bag under his head, coat thrown over him. A murky, reluctant light filtered in from outside.

33

Prague shimmered in the summer sun, clouds of dust artfully rising from under car wheels climbed into the throats of its residents without regard for gender, age, or religious denomination. Prague was the capital of a new country whose name had been the subject of vehement debate for ten years now. Czechs love vehement debates, as long as there's no risk of getting their face smashed in; so this one was right up their alley, nationwide and safe. Bohemia, Czechia, Czechomoravia, Czecho-Moravia? Czechland, Czech Lands, Czecholand? As if changing the name could change the fact that you could live here a hundred years and still meet nothing but idiots, reflected Dyk. Personally, he had no doubt that from a certain, relatively early point in history, the Czech nation had taken on a thoroughly degenerative character, which with the passage of time had intensified into its present-day form. And if the world was up shit creek, Dyk's belief was that the Czechs had played the role of trailblazers in the field: rectum, anus, intestine, esophagus—landscapes known intimately to each and every Czech.

The capital numbered 1,169,106 souls—that is, if we attribute a soul to every inhabitant, in accordance with Christian doctrine, albeit sharply at odds with Dyk's views.

Viktor Dyk turned onto Dobrovsky Street. A child crouched, drawing an outline on the sidewalk, thus adhering to our novel's subtle leitmotiv (witty jokes and doodlings of every sort) and un-intentionally hastening to the aid of literary critics, who, after all, need to earn a living, too.

Dyk stabbed his cane into a dog dropping drying peacefully to the side of the hopscotch grid, and discreetly shook it off into the semicircle called Heaven.

The ex-tavern The Sycamore, now the restaurant Good Living, was located on the corner of Hussite and Veleslavin. The hobnailed single-wing door, with its steel frame and guard plate, gave it the appearance of a nuclear bunker. Two signs hung on the door, one enamel, the other of handmade cardboard construction. The first announced, in a looping retrofont, GOOD FOOD, GOOD LIVING!; the other warned, TOURISTS FLEECED HERE. Guests found it amus-ing, and it didn't prevent the owner from fleecing tourists at all. In fact just the opposite: the unambiguity of the statement elevated the banal bleeding of suckers to the level of patriotic enterprise. Especially since it made tourists, recognizing the word despite its Slavic inflection, come rushing into the pub almost by reflex. "Tourist, turist, yes, jawohl, si!" they would shout as they burst through the door.

As for the locals, the warning gave them the pleasant illusion that they were safe there.

As Dyk stepped into the dining room, Lebeda waved to him from a table by the window. In front of him stood a glass of min-eral water and a plate of spaghetti, which he nibbled circumspectly, unaware that in reality he was glutting himself with slow sugars.

"Forgive me for not waiting," he said as Dyk removed his hat and took a seat in the empty chair. "I did so much running around this morning, I burned off my breakfast a good hour sooner than usual."

"You did the right thing," replied Dyk. "I'm at least twenty minutes late."

A gaunt, elderly waiter shuffled up to their table and wearily tossed down a menu. "Beer?" he rasped.

"I'd like a glass of red," said Dyk. "Have you got anything good?"

"Merlot or Merlot," the plate slinger replied, visibly enjoying the chance to put down one of those provocateurs who ask idiotic questions and act like the restaurant belongs to them.

Though put down, Dyk did not intend to be thrown.

"I'll have the Merlot."

The soup jockey shuffled off.

"I'm glad we were able to meet in such an informal setting," said Lebeda.

The two of them made a comical pair. Lebeda was a giant, or at least a hulk; next to him, Dyk seemed stunted and unhealthy. Lebeda had a round face, wide nose, thick eyebrows, and a fair amount of hair for his age; Dyk's face was vertically aligned, the tip of his nose drooping toward his upper lip, and his head had one less hair on it than *Max, who had only one hair*, and who *Comanche the redskin aimed to scalp while he was laying railroad track.*

"It isn't often one gets to dine with a police commissioner," said Dyk.

"Inspector."

"It's like being in a book."

"Life is a bit like a novel, don't you think?"

"A novel written by life itself."

"Yes."

"Fed into the author's pen by destiny."

"Precisely."

"That's destiny for you."

"You're right. Life is like a book."

"How else could it be."

"Some books are actually fatal."

"And others are fateful."

"Of course. That too."

"Why, even shameful."

"You know, I'm really not that big a reader," said Lebeda hypocritically. "Though I do pick up a book now and then. I recently read *The Memoirs of Juan Caramuel of Lobkowicz*. Newly reissued. Interesting little book."

Dyk was just about to respond—the conversation very much appealed to him so far—when his glass of wine appeared in front of him.

"Are you ready to order?"

Dyk peered at the menu.

"One more minute."

Inspector Lebeda, who had meanwhile finished eating, pushed away his plate, wiped his mouth with his napkin, and lighted his pipe.

"No smoking here."

"No? Then what's this ashtray for?"

"Someone must've put it there," growled the waiter.

"Clearly," retorted Lebeda.

Dyk liked him more every minute. He nearly laughed out loud.

"Chicken medallions à la Chung-Fu," ordered Dyk.

Putting himself at the mercy of more or less serious digestive upsets. The dish steams, the gut screams.

But to hell with it.

"And I'd like something sweet. But I'll wait till my friend here is done." Lebeda puffed on his pipe while the waiter puffed up with rage. It's all a question of verb.

"I propose we drop the 'inspector,'" the inspector went on as the plate slinger walked away in a huff. "Why don't we just chat. After all, I'm new to the neighborhood. You know it, I don't."

"You can say that again. Fifty-five years I've lived here."

"You see? I wasn't even alive yet when you got here."

"It's not your fault," offered Dyk politely.

"Who knows? There are things we'll never know that we could have influenced."

"Don't be so hard on yourself," said Dyk, overdoing it.

"I'm not, actually. But what about you? You moved here after the war. But you also lived in Prague before. You were born here."

"Who told you that?"

"I don't know. I read it somewhere. Or maybe I saw it on TV . . ."

"I grew up in Brevnov. In a villa with a garden. But the Communists took it away. The apartment I'm in now used to belong to my late wife."

"My sincere condolences."

"It's not so bad. Two rooms, a bath, and a kitchen."

"That's not what I meant."

"Me either."

The two of them laughed like old friends.

"Why do you ask, though?"

"Well, I was reassigned here recently. I assume I'll be here a year or so, and I'd like to get some idea what it's like. At first glance it seems pretty calm, but looks can be deceiving, you know."

"Any cases?"

"Seems we've traded places. I'm supposed to be the one asking the questions. But yes, there have been a few recently."

A plate of steaming rice with yellowy bits of meat and something greenish in it landed in front of Dyk with a clatter.

"Anything serious?"

The meal looked like baby rhinoceros vomit.

"Assuming, of course, that it's not a state secret."

Dyk stabbed his fork into a piece of fowl flesh.

"It depends what you mean by serious. Generally people think something's serious when it happens to them, or could have. A car crash is more serious than a murder, since people think murder won't happen to them. A murder may be dramatic, but it isn't serious."

"There haven't been any murders in the neighborhood that I'm aware of."

"That was just an example."

"Oh, I see. State secret."

"Let's just say I'm bound to silence on ongoing cases. But there is one I can tell you about that landed on my desk recently. The statute lapsed on it years ago. A forty-year-old murder from the Ore Mountains. You know the area?"

"Sure, I went camping there a few times when I was young. Like everyone else in those days."

"On that TV show they said that you met your wife on a hiking trip. But they didn't say where."

"That was none of their business. But you mentioned a murder."

"Oh, yes. The unsolved case. Young woman, sixteen stab wounds. Though the doctor thought that was just the murderer's way of confusing the investigators, so they'd think it was a maniac. But apparently the wounds were inflicted calmly and deliberately, with no sign of mental disturbance on the part of the murderer. Only one of the wounds was fatal, the first or second probably. It took place in an isolated location near Bear Rock. The culprit was never found."

"And you're trying to find him now, forty years later?"

"A few days before the murder, some rare prints disappeared from the monastery in Osek. Including some incunabula. Vanished into thin air, and never seen again since—as far as we know. But supposedly somebody saw the young woman in Osek around that time."

"So why look for him now? You said yourself the statute had lapsed."

"Mainly I just want to understand. Comprehend. Occupational hazard, you know. But let's talk about you. Are you writing anything new?"

"Please! At my age?" Dyk felt his right upper denture slowly but surely coming unglued. "That's best left to the young." He jacked it up with his fork and shifted his food to the other side of his mouth.

"So what about your son? They say the apple doesn't fall far from the tree."

"It depends. This one fell pretty far."

"I don't mean to be indiscreet."

"Not at all. He can hardly get out a sentence, let alone write."

"Does he live in Prague?"

"On the outskirts."

"Married?"

"Living together."

"That's common these days. Children?"

"None. As far as I know."

"I don't have any either. But I'm a bachelor. We're probably the same age, aren't we? Your son and I? I'll be forty-six in January."

"That's right. But listen, you're honestly wasting your time on a forty-year-old murder?"

"Just on the side, when there's time left over. I've got a weakness for these things, you know? Unsolved crimes, rebuses, brainteasers, chess problems, that sort of thing. Do you play chess?"

Dyk set down his fork and clacked his dentures shut.

"Not really."

"I used to play some. When I was young. Just for fun, though; I was nothing earthshaking."

"That makes two of us. I knew how to move the pieces, but that was as far as it went."

"Then I dropped it. Went through sort of a peacenik phase. Youth, pacifism, you know? Chess is war. Two armies squaring off, archers, knights, pawns . . ."

"I wouldn't say war."

"No?"

"More like slaughter."

"You'll have to explain."

"A chess match isn't about defeating an army, crushing an enemy. The goal is to murder the king. It's the only way you can win, there's no other path to victory. It's either/or."

"Yes. That's one way to look at it."

"Check mate: 'The king is dead.' It comes from Persian. Theoretically, it can be done in two moves."

"Two? I thought four, at least."

"Two. If you're black."

"I see you got further than I did. Do you still play?"

Dyk smiled.

"Never. That all comes from reading."

He raised his glass.

"To your health, Inspector."

"Mr. Lebeda."

"Mr. Lebeda."

"To your health, Mr. Dyk. Cheers," said Lebeda. "And I hope you won't hold it against me for being so blunt, but I'm glad to have had the chance to get to know you. You're a true gentleman."

"Even the most hardened of criminals would turn gentle in your company."

"I mean that seriously."

"As do I. You aren't so bad yourself."

"Do you ever go to the symphony?"

"More to the theater. But less and less these days. Sitting too long isn't good for me."

As if to prove his point, Dyk uttered a groan of pain, squirmed in his seat, and stretched his legs into the space between the tables.

"I see you have new shoes," said Lebeda with a smile.

"Well, you know," Dyk said vaguely. "I'm still not used to them."

"I realize this may be an inappropriate question, but would you mind telling me how much they cost?"

"I don't remember," lied Dyk. "Keeping a budget was never my strong point. You know, my wife took care of the bills all those years, till I became a widower. I collect my pension the seventh, buy what I feel like buying, and never give it a second thought. Would you care to step on them?"

"Gladly. That movie must have made you a lot of money."

"A couple hundred, yes. Right or left?"

"Left," Inspector Lebeda said. "It's closer to the heart."

And he stepped on Mr. Dyk's new clodhopper.

34

Meanwhile Benedikt Sverak stood in a half-empty pub called Adam's, a glass of something in his hand, observing a couple at the opposite end of the bar. He had latched on to them barely half an hour earlier at the Hotel Zbraslav. The man was probably thirty-five or so, the woman ten years less, give or take. Sverak quivered with pride and excitement: this was quite possibly the case of his life, by virtue of which he would enter the annals of not only crime-solving history, but history as such; perhaps even national history. In his free hand he clutched a crumpled slip of paper that read: *Zbraslav, downtown oasis. City woman with heels, tits, owns holy weapons. Adam, Bedouin buyer. Lay groundwork, write agreement, hide inside peanut dish.*

He'd arrived at the text through a combination of several traditional decryption methods and more or less complex algorithms, applied to a list of antiadvertising slogans that he'd copied on the sly from a folder on Lebeda's desk. Sverak's theory was as follows: what if all the antiadvertising graffiti popping up in the capital of late was actually a series of coded messages from Muslim terrorists planning an assassination in retaliation for the heroic assistance the Czech Republic had so selflessly provided to its allies in Iraq? A bold theory, to be sure, but not entirely dumb: communicating in the language of one's enemy, in plain sight, was a far more effective safeguard than some encrypted Internet babble, no matter how well devised.

In any case Sverak had mined several leads from the graffiti. And one of them had led him here.

The man at the other end of the bar was clearly of Semitic, albeit non-Jewish, origin (in which case the conspiracy would have been much more widespread than Sverak had initially believed). Light gray, classic-cut pinstripe suit, blue silk tie, socks of the same color, yellow patent leather shoes, round black glasses, folding cane for the blind.

The woman was your classic everyday pan-Slavic bimbo.

Sverak swayed between joy at his own savviness—which from all indications had produced undeniable and, at this point, near-tangible results—and fear that he had perhaps bitten off more than he could chew. As a result of which he forgot the cardinal rule of his trade and gawked at the pair so blatantly that even the blindest of blind men would have noticed, never mind a fake one. The man leaned toward his companion and exchanged some words with her. The bimbo glanced at Sverak and said something back. Then the two of them got up and made for the door marked WC. Sverak followed them in. As he shut the door behind him, he hesitated a moment. He suddenly realized he was acting like a total chump. But before he could shape this fleeting thought into slightly more coherent form and draw from it some conclusions to be shot from his brain at lightning speed to the relevant parts of his body, he saw sparks before his eyes and everything went black. The last words he heard in this vale of tears were delivered in pure Praguese:

"You sure it's him?"

"Well, no, not a hundred percent."

Oh Man, thou mirror of debasement! Mucus and gall, time's spoils, departing wayfarer!

35

Mr. Platzek lay in bed, trying to focus his thoughts. He remembered that he was still alive but couldn't remember why. Until a few years ago, he had never had such thoughts, but now everything was different. Ever since the dawn of the new millennium, he had been feeling increasingly uneasy.

There is nothing a priori logical about being alive. Ergo, to ask, along with Mr. Platzek, why Mr. Platzek is alive is itself illogical. Although if a certain degree of elementary logic is essential for the existence of life in space-time, and if there is likewise nothing particularly logical about being alive, then another question presents itself: Is Mr. Platzek real? In reality is Mr. Platzek not but a mere self-delusion—an immaterial cog in a gigantic transhuman simulation of which we have all been virtual victims from the infancy of time?

Friends!

Let us fear not unpleasant questions!

Are we real?

It is no easy thing to arrive at irrefutable conclusions on the matter. The negative hypothesis is in any case not unlikely. Quite the opposite! Disregarding the fact that the ability to doubt our existence is the sole, however tenuous, proof that our existence exists. However, the underlying principle of every functionalist philosophy—the independence of consciousness on the material substratum—teaches us that our existence can't do without us; without ourselves, we don't exist!

Yes, friends! So we stand, unstable and irremediable, on the threshold of a new age.

Ah, Twentieth Century! Dear, dear Twentieth Century! Where will it all end? Marxism! Psychoanalysis! Structuralism! Semiotics! Such lovely, lovely paradigms! Marxism revealed the meaning of history, psychoanalysis exposed the causes of human behavior, structuralism unearthed the roots of myth, and semiotics put labels on it all! But today? What can you be sure of today? Soon, not even your own death!

To be sure, Mr. Platzek thought in categories less abstract than these, which we use here in the melancholy hope of elevating the cultural level of our readers. But be that as it may, the numeral two at the beginning of the current year made Mr. Platzek feel more vulnerable than all the venous ulcers at the local retirees' home combined. So many things changed in the course of a human life! Electricity in every village! Television in every household! And behold, what was modern yesterday is archaic today, and what was crazy yesterday is modern nowadays. Who can keep track of it all? Deutschland befreit Europa! Up with the Soviet Union! In aufrichtiger Mitarbeit! Merrily, merrily goes the worker to the factory! Auf Kriegsdauer geschlossen für den Sieg des Reiches! Back in five minutes! To the machines! Proletarier aller Länder! No pasarán! Human rights!

Or look at China, Lord Almighty! Yesterday a bunch of backward hicks, today the armed fist of neoliberalism. What about that? One end of history's barely over and the next one's already here. And black people all over the streets! He saw one just the other day!

He was torn from his reverie by the ringing of the phone.

"Yes?"

"Mr. Platzek?" a man's voice said.

"Yes?"

"You don't know me, but I've got good news for you."

". . . ?"

"A very attractive offer. What do you say I stop over right now?"

"Now?" Mr. Platzek said, puzzled.

"I'm calling from a cell phone across the street. I'll be over in a minute."

The receiver clicked. Mr. Platzek put on his clothes but didn't have time to gargle. His mouth stank like a pigsty.

"As I was saying, a very attractive offer," said the man. "Fiala's my name. Rudolf Fiala." Crooked teeth, rabbity overbite. Jacket and tie, green corduroys. Youth down the drain and a long way to go to retirement. Beginning baldness. New-looking briefcase.

"What would you say if I offered you one hundred thousand, right here, right now?"

Mr. Platzek, interest piqued, looked up at his visitor.

"Yes, you heard right. I'll lay down a hundred thousand crowns, right on the spot, right here on your table."

Mr. Platzek took his time. His stomach was growling.

"Now tell me, for real: Did you ever expect something like this? Did you think last night when you went to bed that you'd wake up this morning a rich man?"

Mr. Platzek shook his head. He was getting hungrier by the minute.

"So now you're wondering, what do I want from you in exchange for that hundred thousand crowns?"

Mr. Platzek kept quiet.

"Why, my dear sir, nothing! Nothing at all except that rundown shack of yours in the Ore Mountains, which you didn't expect to come into anyway, you don't have any sentimental attachment to it, and even the nuttiest Dutchman wouldn't offer you even a third of what I'm proposing."

"Have a seat," said Mr. Platzek. "I'm going to make some breakfast."

The visitor didn't have a seat. He followed Mr. Platzek into the kitchen.

"Now maybe you think I've lost my mind. Or that this is some kind of joke. Why on earth would anyone give you a hundred thousand crowns for free?"

Mr. Platzek opened the cupboard above the kitchen counter and took out a cup and a plate.

"You're thinking, another one of those crooks trying to launder his dirty money. Or, he must be trying to get rid of some counterfeit bills."

He ran some water into the kettle and turned on the gas.

"Nothing like that, Mr. Platzek. Nothing like that at all."

He opened another cupboard and took out a can of coffee.

"I'll tell you what this is about."

He opened the icebox.

"Because if I don't, you're going to think I'm either a con man or a lunatic."

Inside were a dumpling loaf and two wedges of processed cheese.

"A hundred thou, no joke, absolutely free."

Unsweetened condensed milk, three eggs, and some butter.

"The whole thing's legal. Totally on the up and up. I want to turn your shack into a hotel for foreigners."

A pot with some sort of sauce in it.

"Germans and Dutch, you know what I mean."

Now where is the bread?

"I knock down that wreck of yours, put up something solid, hook up the water and electricity, lay in a driveway, add a parking lot, pool, and a golf course. You know the drill."

In the basket on the table.

"That all costs lots of money. Which I have and you don't. You don't have the funds to invest in something like this. I do."

He took a knife out of the drawer, cut himself a slice of bread, and smeared it with processed cheese.

"So what do you say? One hundred thousand, right here and now."

The water was trying to boil.

"Right here on the spot, honest-to-goodness Czech crowns. No contract, no notary. Just trust and a handshake, man to man."

Mr. Platzek shook some coffee into the cup and poured water over it.

"Just sign here to acknowledge receipt of one hundred thousand Czech crowns and you can go straight out and drink it away."

Two teaspoons of milk and voilà, it was done.

"So? Shall we shake on it?"

Mr. Platzek took a sip from the cup and burned his lips.

"What are you talking about?" he said. "Receipt? Shack? Dutch? I'm an old man. I don't understand these modern things. You must have me confused with someone else."

36

Such a strange, strange building! Windows tinted green like the walls of some aquarium full of gymnodonts aimlessly gliding around, equipped with four limbs and stripped of gills by Darwin's theory. Strange building, strange tenants! Feeble limbs, feeble brains, mollusks dwelling in the twilight of animal evolution; here and there the glow of a television screen, the flare of a lit cigarette, the phosphorescence of putrid bodies in coitus. Next to the strange building, more strange buildings. Across the street, a hideous one-floor convenience store and then more of the same.

The whole thing together was known as the Gagarin Apartments.

Vilém Lebeda sat in the armchair in his living room, sipping visco. For the first time in his life he had purchased a bottle of alcohol without having been invited to a party. Yet he didn't think to marvel at this; he just sat there and drank like the last alcoholic on earth. He had a tough day behind him: a dozen long phone calls, including three long-distance and one international, to the Budapest police; several faxes; dispatching police to various addresses; reading reports. The Linden Street office had come alive with unprecedented commotion; at first his subordinates were unpleasantly surprised, but after a few hours they succumbed to the excitement; for once they'd have something to tell their wives, their lovers, the guys at the pub.

Today Vilém Lebeda had received the facts he'd been missing. They had fallen into place, one by one, like the pieces of a jigsaw puzzle; it all fit, it all tied in, it was all plain and simple. He had just had to step in the right direction for the inexplicable and incongruent to coalesce into a clear and logical pattern. The answer was definitive and murderously clear. He should have thought of it ages ago. Mr. Platzek had unwittingly supplied him with the first clue: "If I had a daughter and she messed around . . ."

Now Lebeda could relax: rattling off Mendeleev's table of the elements, reciting poems from *A Difficult Hour*, trying to recall *Voices of Our Birds*—chi-chi-ri-chi-chi, si-ki-ki—remembering his mother and his rachitic fifth-floor neighbor, slowly sinking into drunkenness, not that I'd kill her, mind you, don't go getting the wrong idea. Mother was right, people come in all sorts, a-ess 33, cee-o 27, if only I'd learned to play chess properly instead of taking the violin, I would have, I coulda figured it out ages ago, whoo-whoo-whoo. What you learn when you're young, you spit out when you're old. What *was* her first name, anyway? Tweet, tweet, tweedle-dee-deet. Love is a mighty enchantress, you can tell a bird by its short hairs, why did I get myself into this? Queen takes on gee-4! Queen e-2! There's no other way, tovarishch, no other way! But Queen aitch-3 and his bird has flown. And took his short hairs with him. Taken. Has taken. Love, the mighty enchantress. Brews poisons, poisons brews. Eat, I should have something to eat. Lebeda stood up and staggered toward the kitchen, but after a few steps changed his mind and turned back. Sinking heavily into his armchair, he seized hold of the teddy bear, laid it on its back; it made a grrring. Two hens on a half-acre and that's all she wrote. A-tee 85. What're we gonna get drunk on? Fluorine, chlorine, bromine, iodine, astatine! Hoy, halogen! Izvinitye mayo plakhoye praizncheniye. Ah, Mr. Dyk, Mr. Dyk, what a wretched writer you are. Érti kérem? Beyond the town, my love, leads a path of white. Igen, uram. Peering at bottom with bleary eyes, he heard this answer, passing wise: Kérem beséljen laszaban! Yet it was clear, clear as a slap in the face, night had clouded his vision forevermore. I am blind! Ar-bee 37, ar-aitch 45, ar-i-pee 1963. Rest in peace! O mine eyes, bow to the lake. What *was* his first name, anyway? His brother. I've got it written down somewhere. Ritten. People come in Al's orts. Alzorts? All sorts. An eye for an eye, a bird in the bush. The bottle was empty.

37

Viktor Dyk poked the ground with his cane, thinking about stage plays that don't have the sense to end when they should. When a line rings out so true that it would be pointless to add anything else, when an actor performs a gesture so perfect the play should come right to an end. Now or never, Dyk said to himself, now is the time; he should let it go while he can. By now our readers have definitively understood that they definitively understand nothing: what could be a more sensible conclusion to our novel than that? Acceptance of fate, acceptance of one's lot, acceptance of one's imperfection. How simple, how biblical! Of making many books there is no end; much study is a weariness of the flesh. Yes! We are born into a novel whose meaning escapes us, and depart from a novel we have never once understood. Now or never! The author has established with his customary skill that he is equally at home in any genre; he has piled plot twist upon plot twist without so much as a second thought; stacked varying styles side by side; stung readers with bitingly sarcastic asides and trenchant social critique; and generously tossed in a thumbnail psychological sketch. Now or never! No one's understood a thing, and even if they had, they could never put me away at my age. There are laws about that. But no: the play goes on, the novel goes on, life goes on; clumsy, pointless, not entertaining at all. Anyone can tell that the best is already behind them, yet they squat there in their seats like perfect idiots, right up until the end, instead of hightailing it for the exit so they won't have to wait for their coats.

38

Mr. Platzek was in a rush, which for him amounted to moving at 1.6 kilometers per hour instead of his customary 1.3. Anyone not in the know would have failed to notice anything unusual, but then, one of the novelist's roles is to let the reader in on confidential information.

Mr. Platzek was in a rush. Something had occurred to him that morning, something about something he had been pondering for nearly a week, ever since the unexpected death of Mrs. Horak. He had known her a relatively long time, even if only casually. She wasn't a regular visitor to the bench; when her rheumatism allowed it, she preferred to stroll in the park—alone or with Mr. Dyk, whose legs still served him well, no matter how much he denied it.

But know her or not, at his age a person couldn't be choosy, as every death was a welcome intrusion into his otherwise by and large meaningless days.

As it happened, shortly before her death, Mr. Platzek had run into Mrs. Horak in the convenience store. They had walked home together with their purchases, Mrs. Horak telling him first about her daughter, then something about the Ore Mountains and some rock or other with bears. Mr. Platzek was positive that the name Dyk had come up. But in connection to what?

He recalled the conversation as soon as he heard about Mrs. Horak's death, and ever since then it had been boring a hole in his head. Until this morning.

Mr. Platzek shuffled his way down to Roosevelt Avenue and was just about to cross when a procession of about thirty-five strong in number came pouring out from the next street. Some waving signs, others wielding blow-up balloons, and still others brandishing posters declaring *Say yes to life, Do you want to be guilty of murder?* and *We demand a ban on abortions.*

There was a time when an infinitely larger procession had come this way, heading for the monument to Generalissimo Stalin, where the first secretary of the mother of parties was giving a speech. Citizens of productive age carried children on their shoulders, outfitted with signs and balloons, while childless citizens carried banners and shouted slogans, radiating determination (firm or unshakable) and serenity (unshakable or firm).

That was in the days when the present belonged to the future and vice versa. Who would have guessed how quickly the slogans would grow old? After the Czechoslovak people overthrew the oppressive regime to the forceful ringing of keys, it became clear that the future, as embodied in the present, belonged chiefly to the past: it was merely a matter of time.

Wherefore, friends, carpe diem! And we will now return to our story.

One young man turned to Mr. Platzek and stuck a flier under his nose titled *Citizens' Petition.*

"Do you know how many abortions are performed in this country each year?" he hostilely inquired.

This perplexed Mr. Platzek—partly because he had no idea, partly because he was afraid if he started a conversation he would forget the something on account of which he had been rushing through the streets for the last ten minutes at the expense of a growing pain in his chest. As a result, he rather gruffly pushed away the hand holding the paper and determinedly forged ahead.

"So you're one of them!" the young man squawked. "Murderer!"

"Murderer!" the crowd cried.

"How many have you killed?" the young man shrieked.

"Devil's servant!" the crowd chanted.

"Satan's accomplice!" the young man went on.

"Accomplice!" the crowd repeated.

"For shame!" the young man continued.

"Shame!" the crowd paraphrased.

"Just wait till you face the Almighty!"

"You'll be in for it then!"

"And it'll be too late!"

"Too late!"

Mr. Platzek had nearly reached the sidewalk. If he didn't get there soon, Mr. Dyk would be gone for lunch. Trying to lengthen his stride, Mr. Platzek miscalculated. One foot tripped on the curb, the other got tangled up with his cane, and he would have fallen flat on his face if a young person of the female persuasion, wearing a low-cut shirt and muddied skirt, hadn't leaped in at the last minute.

"Just leave him alone, lady!" hollered the young man from the other side of the street. "He got what he had coming!"

"God's mills!" the crowd rejoiced.

Mr. Platzek leaned on his rescuer, wheezing gratefully.

"Do you need help?"

Mr. Platzek shook his head.

"Are you hurt?"

Mr. Platzek shook his head.

"Should I call an ambulance?"

Mr. Platzek shook his head.

"Do you want me to walk you home?"

Mr. Platzek shook his head.

And said:

"It's nothing, miss. I was just startled. Thank you very much."

Viktor Dyk, meanwhile, a short distance away, gathered himself up from the bench, wondering what he would have for lunch. Maybe a wiener and mashed potatoes. Or mashed potatoes topped with a fried egg. Or just a wiener. Or scrambled eggs with onion. But first he would go to the church; at this time of day, there wouldn't be a soul.

Suddenly, shooting across the square toward him came a tall man with ruddy cheeks and the air of a foreigner. He had on brown lederhosen, a short-sleeved red shirt, and a Tyrolean hat, with a fagbag around his waist and a camera over his shoulder.

"Do you speak English?" he asked.

"Nein."

"Sprechen Sie Deutsch?" the foreigner inquired cheerfully.

"Nein."

"Ach so." The disappointment in his voice was palpable. "Andy Warhol, it's here? El museo?"

Smiling, Dyk said:

"On meeting a German, I crush him like vermin."

"Bitte?"

Dyk elaborated:

"Chronicle of Dalimil."

"Chronic?"

Running the words through his head, the German arrived at a wholly mistaken conclusion. He pointed to the Andy Warhol Museum and asked:

"Die Gemeindearchive?"

"Nein. Die Gemeindepolizei."

"Die Polizei?"

"Ja. Die Rohlinge. Bestien. Mörder."

The German gazed thoughtfully for a moment at the smiling Dyk, then hesitantly repeated:

"Sprechen Sie Deutsch?"

"Nein."

The tourist awkwardly went on his way.

Now the whole place is going to stink of cologne, thought Dyk. As if there weren't enough cretins around here already.

By the time Mr. Platzek limped to the square, the bench was already empty. He paused a moment, wondering whether or not he should rest. Finally, he dismissed the idea, turned around, and hobbled off. In any case he had forgotten what it was he wanted to tell Mr. Dyk. Something about a rock. But what? He'd probably remember when he got home.

Dyk sat in the first pew, savoring the cool of the church. It wouldn't be long before some joint or other would start to hurt, but he could last a couple of minutes.

A nearly life-size Virgin Mary sat beneath the pulpit. Palms pressed to her breast, head bowed, smiling blissfully. Joseph stood at her right hand with a quizzical look on his face. The plaster was chipped in places, making it look like he had pox on his cheeks and crumbs in his beard. An empty cradle stood between the two of them. Baby Jesus had been stolen. Either that or he'd made a break for it while he still had a chance.

The church was consecrated to Saint Lucy, patron saint of cut-
lers and the blind. She stood in an apse on the right. In one hand
she held a lantern, in the other a dish with two eyes. Which, some
time ago, had inspired Dyk to invent a new game. He took from his
pocket a small pouch of large marbles, purchased in a nearby toy
store that morning, bent over and poured them out on the floor.
The marbles skipped across the uneven stones in every direction.
Dyk stood up and made for the exit, being careful not to step on a
marble and break his skull. Saint Martha stood with a broom by the
door. Try and sweep that up, you sacred cow, Dyk said to himself.
Cheerily he stepped out the door, descended the stairs, and went
home. His soul was at peace.

39

"Look, let's make this quick," said Lieutenant Valach. "Do you confess?"

"To what?"

"Did you rape her, yes or no?"

"Well, maybe. But just a little."

"What do you mean, a little?"

"I was only in her for a second. Hardly at all."

"So you confess?"

"You could put it that way. With one proviso."

"You can take that up in court."

"You bet I will. No doubt about it. But I want you to put it in my confession. One proviso. Otherwise I won't sign. You can sign it yourself. Just like Munich in '38. About us without us. I couldn't care less."

That was on Tuesday afternoon. Martin Valach was filling in for Sverak, who had requested three days off. Lebeda had phoned in sick that morning. It was still sweltering hot, with nothing to suggest that it would let up anytime soon. The minister of health was recommending that older people drink a lot of water, even if they weren't thirsty.

40

The next day, Mr. Platzek fell out the window. As it happened, he smeared himself on the sidewalk without injuring any pedestrians. The citizens quickly crowded around the lifeless body.

"Ah!"

"Oh!"

"Pardon me!"

"Move it!"

"Excuse me!"

"Hey!"

"Good Lord!"

"Who is it?"

"Do you know him?"

"That idiot! He could have killed someone!"

"What idiot? That's Mr. Platzek!"

"As if he couldn't have jumped out the window at night!"

"Get those children out of here! Get those kids away!"

"Just like under the Communists! Poor guy, I bet they were trying to evict him."

"That's no reason to jump in broad daylight!"

"Call an ambulance!"

"Call the police!"

"Ambulance? More like a shovel!"

"Does anyone here have a cell phone?"

"Get that dog out of here!"

PATRIK OUŘEDNÍK was born in Prague, but emigrated to France in 1984, where he still lives. He is the author of twelve books, including fiction, essays, and poems. He is also the Czech translator of novels, short stories, and plays from such writers as François Rabelais, Alfred Jarry, Raymond Queneau, Samuel Beckett, and Boris Vian. He has received a number of literary awards for his writing, including the Czech Literary Fund Award.

ALEX ZUCKER's translation of Jáchym Topol's *City Sister Silver* (2000) was selected for inclusion in the 2006 guide *1001 Books You Must Read Before You Die*. He lives in Brooklyn.

PETROS ABATZOGLOU, *What Does Mrs. Freeman Want?*
MICHAL AJVAZ, *The Golden Age.*
The Other City.
PIERRE ALBERT-BIROT, *Grabinoulor.*
YUZ ALESHKOVSKY, *Kangaroo.*
FELIPE ALFAU, *Chromos.*
Locos.
IVAN ÂNGELO, *The Celebration.*
The Tower of Glass.
DAVID ANTIN, *Talking.*
ANTÓNIO LOBO ANTUNES, *Knowledge of Hell.*
ALAIN ARIAS-MISSON, *Theatre of Incest.*
JOHN ASHBERY AND JAMES SCHUYLER, *A Nest of Ninnies.*
HEIMRAD BÄCKER, *transcript.*
DJUNA BARNES, *Ladies Almanack.*
Ryder.
JOHN BARTH, *LETTERS.*
Sabbatical.
DONALD BARTHELME, *The King.*
Paradise.
SVETISLAV BASARA, *Chinese Letter.*
MARK BINELLI, *Sacco and Vanzetti Must Die!*
ANDREI BITOV, *Pushkin House.*
LOUIS PAUL BOON, *Chapel Road.*
My Little War.
Summer in Termuren.
ROGER BOYLAN, *Killoyle.*
IGNÁCIO DE LOYOLA BRANDÃO, *Anonymous Celebrity.*
Teeth under the Sun.
Zero.
BONNIE BREMSER, *Troia: Mexican Memoirs.*
CHRISTINE BROOKE-ROSE, *Amalgamemnon.*
BRIGID BROPHY, *In Transit.*
MEREDITH BROSNAN, *Mr. Dynamite.*
GERALD L. BRUNS, *Modern Poetry and the Idea of Language.*
EVGENY BUNIMOVICH AND J. KATES, EDS., *Contemporary Russian Poetry: An Anthology.*
GABRIELLE BURTON, *Heartbreak Hotel.*
MICHEL BUTOR, *Degrees.*
Mobile.
Portrait of the Artist as a Young Ape.
G. CABRERA INFANTE, *Infante's Inferno.*
Three Trapped Tigers.
JULIETA CAMPOS, *The Fear of Losing Eurydice.*
ANNE CARSON, *Eros the Bittersweet.*
CAMILO JOSÉ CELA, *Christ versus Arizona.*
The Family of Pascual Duarte.
The Hive.
LOUIS-FERDINAND CÉLINE, *Castle to Castle.*
Conversations with Professor Y.
London Bridge.
Normance.
North.
Rigadoon.
HUGO CHARTERIS, *The Tide Is Right.*
JEROME CHARYN, *The Tar Baby.*
MARC CHOLODENKO, *Mordechai Schamz.*

JOSHUA COHEN, *Witz.*
EMILY HOLMES COLEMAN, *The Shutter of Snow.*
ROBERT COOVER, *A Night at the Movies.*
STANLEY CRAWFORD, *Log of the S.S. The Mrs Unguentine.*
Some Instructions to My Wife.
ROBERT CREELEY, *Collected Prose.*
RENÉ CREVEL, *Putting My Foot in It.*
RALPH CUSACK, *Cadenza.*
SUSAN DAITCH, *L.C.*
Storytown.
NICHOLAS DELBANCO, *The Count of Concord.*
NIGEL DENNIS, *Cards of Identity.*
PETER DIMOCK, *A Short Rhetoric for Leaving the Family.*
ARIEL DORFMAN, *Konfidenz.*
COLEMAN DOWELL, *The Houses of Children.*
Island People.
Too Much Flesh and Jabez.
ARKADII DRAGOMOSHCHENKO, *Dust.*
RIKKI DUCORNET, *The Complete Butcher's Tales.*
The Fountains of Neptune.
The Jade Cabinet.
The One Marvelous Thing.
Phosphor in Dreamland.
The Stain.
The Word "Desire."
WILLIAM EASTLAKE, *The Bamboo Bed.*
Castle Keep.
Lyric of the Circle Heart.
JEAN ECHENOZ, *Chopin's Move.*
STANLEY ELKIN, *A Bad Man.*
Boswell: A Modern Comedy.
Criers and Kibitzers, Kibitzers and Criers.
The Dick Gibson Show.
The Franchiser.
George Mills.
The Living End.
The MacGuffin.
The Magic Kingdom.
Mrs. Ted Bliss.
The Rabbi of Lud.
Van Gogh's Room at Arles.
ANNIE ERNAUX, *Cleaned Out.*
LAUREN FAIRBANKS, *Muzzle Thyself.*
Sister Carrie.
LESLIE A. FIEDLER, *Love and Death in the American Novel.*
JUAN FILLOY, *Op Oloop.*
GUSTAVE FLAUBERT, *Bouvard and Pécuchet.*
KASS FLEISHER, *Talking out of School.*
FORD MADOX FORD, *The March of Literature.*
JON FOSSE, *Melancholy.*
MAX FRISCH, *I'm Not Stiller.*
Man in the Holocene.
CARLOS FUENTES, *Christopher Unborn.*
Distant Relations.
Terra Nostra.
Where the Air Is Clear.

FOR A FULL LIST OF PUBLICATIONS, VISIT:
www.dalkeyarchive.com

JANICE GALLOWAY, *Foreign Parts.*
 The Trick Is to Keep Breathing.
WILLIAM H. GASS, *Cartesian Sonata*
 and Other Novellas.
 Finding a Form.
 A Temple of Texts.
 The Tunnel.
 Willie Masters' Lonesome Wife.
GÉRARD GAVARRY, *Hoppla! 1 2 3.*
ETIENNE GILSON,
 The Arts of the Beautiful.
 Forms and Substances in the Arts.
C. S. GISCOMBE, *Giscome Road.*
 Here.
 Prairie Style.
DOUGLAS GLOVER, *Bad News of the Heart.*
 The Enamoured Knight.
WITOLD GOMBROWICZ,
 A Kind of Testament.
KAREN ELIZABETH GORDON, *The Red Shoes.*
GEORGI GOSPODINOV, *Natural Novel.*
JUAN GOYTISOLO, *Count Julian.*
 Juan the Landless.
 Makbara.
 Marks of Identity.
PATRICK GRAINVILLE, *The Cave of Heaven.*
HENRY GREEN, *Back.*
 Blindness.
 Concluding.
 Doting.
 Nothing.
JIŘÍ GRUŠA, *The Questionnaire.*
GABRIEL GUDDING,
 Rhode Island Notebook.
MELA HARTWIG, *Am I a Redundant*
 Human Being?
JOHN HAWKES, *The Passion Artist.*
 Whistlejacket.
ALEKSANDAR HEMON, ED.,
 Best European Fiction 2010.
AIDAN HIGGINS, *A Bestiary.*
 Balcony of Europe.
 Bornholm Night-Ferry.
 Darkling Plain: Texts for the Air.
 Flotsam and Jetsam.
 Langrishe, Go Down.
 Scenes from a Receding Past.
 Windy Arbours.
ALDOUS HUXLEY, *Antic Hay.*
 Crome Yellow.
 Point Counter Point.
 Those Barren Leaves.
 Time Must Have a Stop.
MIKHAIL IOSSEL AND JEFF PARKER, EDS.,
 Amerika: Russian Writers View the
 United States.
GERT JONKE, *The Distant Sound.*
 Geometric Regional Novel.
 Homage to Czerny.
 The System of Vienna.
JACQUES JOUET, *Mountain R.*
 Savage.
CHARLES JULIET, *Conversations with*
 Samuel Beckett and Bram van
 Velde.
MIEKO KANAI, *The Word Book.*

HUGH KENNER, *The Counterfeiters.*
 Flaubert, Joyce and Beckett:
 The Stoic Comedians.
 Joyce's Voices.
DANILO KIŠ, *Garden, Ashes.*
 A Tomb for Boris Davidovich.
ANITA KONKKA, *A Fool's Paradise.*
GEORGE KONRÁD, *The City Builder.*
TADEUSZ KONWICKI, *A Minor Apocalypse.*
 The Polish Complex.
MENIS KOUMANDAREAS, *Koula.*
ELAINE KRAF, *The Princess of 72nd Street.*
JIM KRUSOE, *Iceland.*
EWA KURYLUK, *Century 21.*
ERIC LAURRENT, *Do Not Touch.*
VIOLETTE LEDUC, *La Bâtarde.*
SUZANNE JILL LEVINE, *The Subversive*
 Scribe: Translating Latin
 American Fiction.
DEBORAH LEVY, *Billy and Girl.*
 Pillow Talk in Europe and Other
 Places.
JOSÉ LEZAMA LIMA, *Paradiso.*
ROSA LIKSOM, *Dark Paradise.*
OSMAN LINS, *Avalovara.*
 The Queen of the Prisons of Greece.
ALF MAC LOCHLAINN,
 The Corpus in the Library.
 Out of Focus.
RON LOEWINSOHN, *Magnetic Field(s).*
BRIAN LYNCH, *The Winner of Sorrow.*
D. KEITH MANO, *Take Five.*
MICHELINE AHARONIAN MARCOM,
 The Mirror in the Well.
BEN MARCUS,
 The Age of Wire and String.
WALLACE MARKFIELD,
 Teitlebaum's Window.
 To an Early Grave.
DAVID MARKSON, *Reader's Block.*
 Springer's Progress.
 Wittgenstein's Mistress.
CAROLE MASO, *AVA.*
LADISLAV MATEJKA AND KRYSTYNA
 POMORSKA, EDS.,
 Readings in Russian Poetics:
 Formalist and Structuralist Views.
HARRY MATHEWS,
 The Case of the Persevering Maltese:
 Collected Essays.
 Cigarettes.
 The Conversions.
 The Human Country: New and
 Collected Stories.
 The Journalist.
 My Life in CIA.
 Singular Pleasures.
 The Sinking of the Odradek
 Stadium.
 Tlooth.
 20 Lines a Day.
ROBERT L. MCLAUGHLIN, ED.,
 Innovations: An Anthology of
 Modern & Contemporary Fiction.
HERMAN MELVILLE, *The Confidence-Man.*
AMANDA MICHALOPOULOU, *I'd Like.*

SELECTED DALKEY ARCHIVE PAPERBACKS

FOR A FULL LIST OF PUBLICATIONS, VISIT:
www.dalkeyarchive.com